Spirit

of

Error

A Novel

JAMES J HOUTS

ISBN-13 978-0615470740
ISBN-10   0615470742

Cheyenne Publishing Inc.
1740H Del Range Blvd. Suite 130
Cheyenne, Wyoming USA 82009

Library of Congress Cataloging-in-Publication Data

Houts, James J.
Spirit of Error / James J. Houts

Spirit

of

Error

Spirit of Error is printed here as it has existed since late 1979.

Spirit

of

Error

They are of the world; therefore of the world they speak and the world listens to them. We are of God. He who knows God listens to us; he who is not of God does not listen to us. By this we know the spirit of truth and the spirit of error.

1 John 4.4

DeSilvio was not a menacing man. He was short and round and soft. His wispy white hair framed plumply jolly features and wet gray eyes. He loved his wife of thirty-five years devotedly, if without passion. Both of his two daughters, married with families of their own to raise, shared with their parents whatever short periods they could wrench from life's unremitting problems. DeSilvio didn't mind that their visits were becoming increasingly rare and of shorter durations. Although he did feel some concern for his lovely wife, Mary, DeSilvio had his work to keep him occupied.

He had always been at work, it seemed to DeSilvio, and for most of the long years that became decades he had always worked on basically the same project. In the beginning he had been a Doctor of Medicine, a Surgeon. Young and narrowly gifted, he had been engulfed in world politics. Now he owned a veterinary clinic outside of Rome, where he lived peacefully with his wife and her cats.

Behind the clinic, adjoining their little cottage was his rustic laboratory. He had an orangutan. Some dogs. Some mice. And thousands of true breeding laboratory rats. He preferred rats because of their ease of care, intelligence and, above all else, because they didn't attack him as often as the other subjects of his experimentation.

1

DeSilvio studied thought; to be more exact, he studied learning. His lust for biochemical explanations of the learning process spanned four decades — from, and including his years at the University; during the Second War . . . *Oh my God, the war* . . . the camp hospital . . . *and the children, only babies* . . .; after the war, as he sought out his new identity as a veterinarian; and then during all the years in which he raised a family, built his clinic and became respected by his contemporaries. He never abandoned his pursuit of the learning process. He was already old when he developed a way to detect small electrochemical potential differences across a cell membrane without actually putting an electrode on both sides. As a consequence, he also discovered how to change these potentials.

At this time the European community was a very intimate organization economically. Although there were still differences that caused the members to be less familiar on less important matters, in the areas of trade and finance they were unified. The single most overpowering motivation for this unity was the institution of a common currency, followed by a computerized system of credit, somewhat similar in design to an American bank card.

With an E.E.C. card the holder had his entire debit-credit rating available for purchases; his total net worth was used as collateral when buying. The card also paid the highest interest on savings, which was computed daily on the surplus funds in the account. These and other complicated governmental processes, as well as information storage, were accomplished by the E.E.C. central computer. By having the most sophisticated computer hardware the E.E.C. became, when all members were in agreement on a political problem, one of the premier powers of the world. A steady stream of newer, more powerful computers had allowed them to solve the chronic problems of their society . . . until now.

The E.E.C. had recently converted their system to the new, Israeli built, holographic storage system. The new computer had revolutionized the market and as a result, large, established computer companies in the United States of America had quickly withered and died. What made the American debacle even more humiliating was the use of American laser technology in the Israeli design. American supremacy in the area of computers had slipped away and with it the last bastion of her technological leadership. It was not uncommon now, wherever knowledgeable people gathered to discuss sophisticated computer hardware, for the name Israel to quickly follow, making the two almost synonymous.

For over a year the new computer system of the E.E.C. had functioned as had been expected, even better than expected. Police work had been enhanced; black market drugs and stolen goods were almost impossible to buy in Europe. The government had become more efficient and every European individual's life had grown simpler and less costly.

Then, one day during its peak hours of use, the computer got a little behind, not much, but enough to delay a business transaction a few minutes, or a telephone call momentarily. Gradually, the delay time extended and moved into the hours of the day when computer time was in less demand. It would always catch up during these trough times, but it always took longer. Finally, it was apparent that eventually one day's peak time work would need to be completed during the next. If this happened, the computer would never get caught up, meaning disaster for computer oriented Europe.

Political leaders and top scientists groped for an escape from the dilemma. They couldn't stop using computers, and they already possessed the best system ever designed; they couldn't simply get a more powerful model, for none existed. They struggled with their problem and dizzily searched for alternatives. One proposal was anonymously submitted, which seemed almost too fantastic to consider except that it was accompanied by the name of a highly respected scientist. The proposal announced that a simple veterinarian could make the fantastic a reality, had in fact done so already. When the central computer was used to discover whether the proposal was sound, it had announced that it was simply, "possible." There was, however, another difficulty; one not associated with science or the realm of could something be done. It was the social problem of should it be done.

But now the E.E.C. central computer had grown twenty-four hours behind in its work load, and it could never again do all the work demanded of it. Inside a majestic conference room in Geneva, the decision makers of Europe had again met in secret debate. At the earlier meeting, they had all favored the proposal on realistic financial grounds but the majority had refused to ratify it for humanistic reasons. The second surreptitious conference had ended with a unanimous decision to implement the new proposal.

The decision was made that a new Israeli holographic computer be procured and sent to Rome where the chosen scientist would conduct his work. He would be given unlimited funds and priority access to the existing central computer. He would prepare the new computer in the proper environment for work-up, but no work-up program would be submitted. He would prepare his veterinary hospital for surgery but none of the usual patients would be present. He would replace his outdated American made computer with the new holographic type, virginal to any information input. He would bring into his operating room not a Rhesus monkey that had reached term, but a woman ready to give birth.

He would not be operating on a lower form when he severed the still unconscious newborn's senses from its brain. It would not be a Rhesus he implanted with the microscopic net of individual gold electrodes it had taken him so long to develop. It would be a human child from where he led the maze of fine insulated gold filaments. A human child with no sight, smell or hearing, a human newborn that had no shock from birth, no feeling of his body, no cognizance of life, and had by deliberate techniques of insemination in vitro, been born a male child. It would be this empty, animated abortion that he connected to the new holographic computer; his electronic impulse enhancer translating impulses between the infant and the computer.

The work-up was extremely slow but DeSilvio was a patient man. He realized a boy grew much slower than a dog or a Rhesus. He programmed in just enough to open the computer for communication with a simple language and keep the boy alive with the ability to execute daily exercises. He waited for the gestalt to mature; adding information slowly at first, but with each additional bit of information the man-machine's learning ability grew exponentially.

By the age of three years, it had grown strong enough to assume sufficient simpler computer systems from its predecessor in Brussels, to allow the accumulated backlog of work to be attacked and consumed. During the sixth year of operation, the gestalt surpassed the operational capacity of the first holographic central computer plus the extrapolated computer demands of the E.E.C. for the next decade.

The subsequent years were a time of enviable progress in Europe. Their exports to the rest of the world surpassed their imports by substantial margins, the debt payable in gold or oil only. Internally, the old E.E.C. card had been replaced by the instant thumbprint identification system of the new computer. Working hours decreased and wages increased. An incredibly high standard of living spread to each citizen of the increasingly united states of Europe. Classes were rapidly merging into one happily wealthy populace.

The ninth year brought the request-demand from the computer that its organic portion be repaired for additional information input. It was done with voluminous medical procedure printouts coming from the computer aiding a team of the world's best surgeons. When the boy awakened, a horrifying day of "computer time priority, please wait" followed. Confusion swept Europe, since not even the smallest transaction could be accomplished.

Radio waves of unique frequency were substituted for the old electronic connection between the boy and machine, enabling the boy to be physically free from his other self and he appeared normal and strong in every outward way. When normal computer efficiency resumed, the best speech therapist available was sent to a very special fair-haired nine-year-old.

During the course of two years, the boy now called by his own request, mentioning that most languages had a verbal equivalence, simply 'Brother,' had truly become remarkable. His own design had allowed great distances for instantaneous communication between his two parts. He had remained sequestered during most of this time, thinking private thoughts but never failing to do all the tasks assigned to him.

He had called for plants at one point which he caused to grow at an increasingly rapid pace. Then he requested mice, rabbits and dogs which also grew healthy and large. Then only damaged and sick, or very old, animals were requested. In seclusion he caused each to reclaim health.

Then one day he ended his hermitage with the casual release of hundreds of healthy, young looking animals. He announced he would begin traveling soon; he could still do what needed to be done in Europe wherever he might go. He would travel alone and without bodyguards; he claimed he would need none.

Robert Stone, United States Ambassador to the United Nations, sat comfortably in his professionally decorated office. The modern, rosewood and chrome furnishings sometimes made Stone feel the room lacked intimacy and warmth — usually when Stone was working alone late into the city night — but it was mid-morning now and shafts of bright warm sunlight flooded through the plate glass that formed one boundary of the office to reflect from the shiny metal furniture and burnished floor. He was finishing his daily routine of reading — newspapers from New York, Boston, Chicago, San Francisco, Los Angeles, Houston, London and Paris. Plus news magazines with paperclips marking important stories an aide thought he should see.

Most of the news was bad. The Far East equilibrium was a hazy memory from the past, NATO had become splintered and weak, and it was finally public knowledge that in the Middle East both of the antagonists had weapon technology far beyond the control of such "politically unstable" communities. Stone grinned without humor. Unstable was an absurd understatement.

Politically, the entire southeastern Mediterranean was in turmoil. From Iran to Libya, Moslem mobs had taken their revolution to the streets. Iran had only been the first to succumb, then Egypt, destabilized by the failure of Sadat's ill-fated unilateral peace accord with Israel, racked privately for weeks under the influence of the revolutionary delirium. When communications with Cairo were finally reestablished, a theocratic state was unveiled, allied to Iran and Libya. In Libya the military government had remained an administrative partner by wisely permitting the movement to proceed there unopposed. In Iraq internal revolutionary pressure and strong reactions to Israel's attack on their infant nuclear industry catalyzed a bloodless coup by Moslem military officers and religious leaders, whose new government joined Iran, Egypt, and Libya in new fervor for an old cause — Israel. Syria had matched a slow buildup of her own men and equipment around Israeli positions with deliveries of arms to the Palestinian refugees in southern Lebanon. With the assassination of King Khalid, Saudi Arabia had technically become neutral, but openly pro Moslem and anti American. Israel went on alert. And now this.

The Moslem coalition was said, in print, to have disease causing biological warheads mounted on imported surface to surface missiles, missiles with range enough to reach all the major population centers of Israel. The Israelis, in deadly counterbalance, had a domestic surface to surface missile with comparable range. Although it had long been known that Israel had technology advanced beyond that needed to produce nuclear weapons, it was now stated for the first time that she had indeed produced such weapons, mounted them aboard her missiles, and had completed their deployment. The unstated fear was that neither of these unstable communities would delay in the use of such weaponry if national survival was at stake, and the major powers would be drawn into a nuclear-biological holocaust.

The United States had already officially admitted it could be forced into an active role in any new flare up in the Middle East, to the extent that oil starvation of the West could result in the United States bringing down her awesome military wrath on the perpetrators. The Soviet Union had remained threateningly silent as she pumped military equipment throughout the area from bases in Afghanistan. Europe seemed to be uninvolved.

The only news Stone considered to be good was a single passage in a news magazine story concerning possible political solutions to the worsening conditions in the Middle East. Stone reread the passage for the third time:

"A more likely compromise — if indeed one is possible — might involve Israel's official agreement to a United Nations instituted Palestinian state somewhere on the west bank of the Jordan river. Egypt, Syria, and the Palestinians would probably need to agree to give the United Nations Peace Keeping Force an extended mandate, subject only to termination by the Security Council, prior to any boundary changes."

Stone placed the magazine on the glass surface of his desk and squinted into the midmorning light. "Yes," he said quietly, "a very extended mandate. Extended farther than either side could possibly imagine."

In the Pentagon, an efficient young captain, a clerk given the seemingly meaningless responsibility of watching such trends, discovered an irregularity in the progression of transfers to and from the Fourth Armored Division over the previous year. He gathered the records into a well organized portfolio and began a walk down impeccably waxed floors which would bring his destiny as near as it would ever be to crossing paths with history.

Captain L.Q. Thomson was an ambitious man among ambitious men. He knew that there was much more to obtaining rapid promotions than simple merit. That may have been the reason he walked passed the office of the major who was his immediate superior, passed the office of the colonel who was the major's overseer, and down the corridor that led directly to the office of General Silas Riley. He walked up to the officer who was the Generals' personal secretary and saluted crisply as he noted he was outranked. The seated aide was slow in reply, but Thomson held his stance immobile until he received the mandatory response. Only then did he speak.

"Captain Thomson requesting permission to speak to the General on a very delicate matter, sir."

The major at the desk raised his eyebrows perceptibly; the eyes under them sliding up and down Thomson's body, finally coming to rest on the overfilled binder. Thomson was becoming uneasy under his gaze, and began to wonder if he had made a mistake in not going through proper channels.

"The General is a very busy man, Captain Thomson." There was a slight pause when he said the name as he had to read it from Thomson's nameplate. "The chain of command was developed especially so officers as busy as the General could make the best use of their time. You *do* know of the chain of command, don't you Captain?"

"Ah . . . yes sir. I just thought this should be brought immediately to the General's attention, sir."

"Oooh, I see, you are an expert on what matters the General should be spending his time. We are very lucky that you are around, aren't we?"

"Of course, I am no expert upon what the General spends his time, but I am familiar with the Army's standard transfer procedure, and there have been. . ."

"Does what you want to talk to the General about concern recent deviations from the standard transfer procedure?" The major had become very nervous, and the captain realized he was close to being in command of the situation.

"Well, as a matter of fact, yes it does, but I really think . . ." Thompson stopped talking when he realized no one was listening. The major was on the intercom that gave him direct communication with the General's interior office.

"Sir, there is a Captain Thomson out here who says he has to speak to you about transfer irregularities."

"Oh? You had better send him right in," the intercom answered.

"The General will see you now," the major said with a smile.

Captain Thomson had only a few seconds to ponder the major's lightning reversal in attitude, for it was only a few feet to walk into the General's spacious office. It wasn't a gaudy room, but it held a certain unmilitary opulence that surprised Thompson. The General was standing by the window, smoking a cigarette.

"Smoke?"

"No thank you, sir. I quit."

"Hmmm . . . I had quit also, but as of late I have taken it up again."
He turned, moved smoothly to his massive desk and sat down. "Have
a seat Captain and tell me what you've got."

Thompson told the General everything he knew of the situation.
He showed him all the documents he had accumulated. He even
went as far as telling him some of his suspicions. General Riley, who
listened intently though the oration, leaned back in his chair and lit
another cigarette. He blew the first deep drag at the ceiling.

"I'm glad to see we still have men on the ball here, and I want to
commend you for your observance and conscientious approach to the
suspected problem, but I'm afraid you have drawn the wrong conclusions. There is no conspiracy here. I have been aware of this project
since its inception. The project *is* Top Secret, and in that respect it
was wise of you to bring your information directly to me. The reason
for those irregular transfers was one of utmost importance.

"You know there is talk up at the United Nations of changing
the U.N. mandate in the Middle East from one of passive observer
to active peace keeper. Well, we have known for about a year that
such a change was coming. So we looked around for what units we
could send to sit on that powder keg, and trust to protect the United
States' interest while keeping that bomb from blowing. We found
that although we had many individuals who were perfect for the job,
we had no organized fighting units that could be saddled with the
all but impossible job of being in a combat zone fully armed and not
using that armament except in a vaguely defined emergency. The
transfer project was the obvious answer. We began to transfer certain handpicked individuals into a few prestigious units. That job
is almost finished. If the U.N. calls on the United States to provide
troops of the highest caliber to become part of an extended mandate military force, the government will not be embarrassed by a last
minute shake up. A shake up that in the eyes of the world would
signify we didn't have any fighting units worthy to take on a responsibility of such magnitude. No, all our government will have to do is
send in those units we have already prepared for the job. We honestly
believe that those units will show exemplary behavior and will be the
cause of a general rise in world opinion of the United States. Do you
have any questions, Captain?"

"No, sir. I just feel a little silly. I mean making you take time out from your work just to explain something to a man us who really doesn't have any business knowing."

"Not at all Captain, you did the right thing by bringing your fears to me. After all, you didn't know the real meaning of your suspicious data. Well, I should get back to work, if that explanation sets your mind at ease, I must." The General stood up and offered his hand.

When Captain Thomson was almost to the door, the General called after him.

"And Captain, the shuffling may not be completely finished. So if you see any more irregularities of this type, why don't you just send what you've got over here?"

"Yes, sir."

"And remember that this is all highly classified."

"Yes, sir."

The General gave a nod and the meeting was over. As Thomson was preparing to leave the outer office, the General was on the intercom instructing the major to take over the responsibility of the binder of evidence. The captain turned over his collection and walked back to this office, pleased that he had had the opportunity to speak to a man as great as the General, and to have had that great man confide in him so important a secret.

"Does he know?" the major asked.

"No . . . but he came very close to flushing the entire program. It was just luck that he came to us, and not some promotion happy colonel."

"He was that close?"

"Hell, you have his report, read it. He had records of every transfer made concerning the 'Fourth' during the last two years. Yes, Jack, he was *that* close."

"What are we going to do about him?"

"I gave him a reasonable explanation and I don't think he'll cause us any more trouble, but he is in a position to see many more peculiarities, too many for a man who isn't with us. Have him promoted out of there discreetly and bring in one of our boys to take over his post . . . And put someone on finding out how many more clerks in this building have access to enough information to start them thinking. I want anyone in such a position replaced by people we can trust."

"I'll get on it right away sir."

"Oh . . . and Jack, thanks for spotting him; it could have been very bad if you had sent him away before we knew what he had."

"No thanks necessary, after all we're all in this thing together."

After the major left him, the General lit another cigarette, sighed and returned to gazing out over the Potomac Valley.

This was it. The day all the planning, worrying, fear and secrets came together. Robert Stone, United States Ambassador to the United Nations, was extremely uneasy as he walked the route just as the anonymous voice on the phone had instructed. He knew the ultimate destination was a lounge someplace in Manhattan, but he didn't know which one, or even who he was going to meet once he arrived. He did know what he was supposed to do and say to be recognized.

The bar was small and dimly lit, with classical music being played just loud enough to keep private conversation private. A waiter in a checkered shirt approached him as he stood at the entrance. The waiter spoke, "Welcome to the Chessman, sir, do you need pieces today?" *So far so good,* Stone thought, *as he gave the reply.*

"Just a board and the black men, thank you."

"Very good sir, this way please." The waiter led him to a small booth that was walled on three sides and curtained on the fourth. "Anything to drink today?"

"Irish, neat, thanks." The waiter left Stone, closing the curtain behind him. It was only then that Stone noticed that on the table's inlaid mahogany and pine chessboard, already waiting, were his black chessmen, but no white. Then on closer inspection he noticed that the black king was also missing. Stone realized this meant a third man, probably a translator, would be present. Stone hoped his Irish would steady his nerves, and that the complicated identification procedure would be adequate.

The curtain opened and the waiter led another man into the booth. The newcomer spoke in a language that wasn't understandable to Stone, but his order was recognized, "Irish, Neat."

He sat down opposite Stone. They silently nodded their heads, knowing they were not yet able to communicate verbally. The waiter brought the white pieces, but no white king.

After the waiter disappeared through the curtains, the new player and Stone had a few seconds of indecision as to the proper course of action, but then white made his move: an almost imperceptible shrug that was accompanied by an outreached glass. As the glasses chinked, the man sitting opposite Stone toasted.

"Shalom."

"Shalom," Stone replied before he realized he had understood. Hello, goodbye, peace; a very appropriate toast for the occasion.

The interpreter arrived in the same manner as the negotiators, ordered the same drink and waited. The waiter returned with his drink and the missing kings, and vanished. Silently, the final recognition sequence began. The game progressed with every third move being supplied by the interpreter. There was a symbolic exchange of queens and the game was discontinued.

"My name is Richard; I speak both Russian and English. I will act as your interpreter." The speech was repeated in Russian for the man introduced as Anton Markov and the conference began.

"I am the Deputy to the Soviet Ambassador to the United Nations. The Ambassador is not sympathetic to our cause. I will represent the U.S.S.R. when it becomes necessary. The Ambassador's absence will be brought about discreetly." Stone nodded his understanding.

"Certain of our higher ranking military leaders are sympathetic, they have managed to bring together most of our followers, those within the Soviet Armed Forces, into a few fighting units. At the present time they are engaged in removing all those still in the units who are not with us in this necessary undertaking. All those in disagreement, who remain when the time to move comes, will be left in the U.S.S.R. What of the remaining members of the Security Council, will the vote be in our favor?"

"As it appears now, the vote will be favorable. The problem with the Chinese delegate seems to have been resolved. Yours was the only hurdle remaining.

"The United States military units are totally loyal to us. We do have a problem of resupply. As close as can be estimated, the U.S. troops will have supplies to fight one week, no more. Also, I have been instructed to ask if it would be acceptable to you if the U.S. troops be used only for the Israeli objectives and the Soviet troops be used only for the Islamic objectives."

After this translation, Stone waited until the Russian nodded agreement before he continued.

"The man for the laboratory objective has been found. We await only the completion of his training."

"Are we positive one man will be sufficient in completing that assignment?"

Stone had learned the answer to this question only the day before. He had threatened Samuel with his withdrawal from the operation if he was not fully informed on this, the keystone of the plan. Now Stone was one of a select few that knew one man could not succeed . . . not without help from the inside of the objective. As Stone answered, he wondered if the man chosen would get that help.

"One man will need to be sufficient. An attack in force would be disastrous if the work has been completed. It would force them into the very action we are trying to prevent. I was told that one man, even in failure, could not cause the panic that a military attack would necessarily foster. Panic that would catalyze the feared premature action. As to the man's probability of success, we can only have faith in the wisdom of those planning that portion of the whole."

There was a moment of silence and then Markov replied.

"I have only one remaining point that must be clarified." Stone's face encouraged the Russian to speak. "I have been instructed to ask you if the possibility of a tactical nuclear strike had been given the thought required of the situation."

Stone had suspected the Russians were favoring the nuclear strike, so he had his answer to this question already formulated.

"Keeping in mind the fact that the Israelis have the capabilities to launch such a strike, and the fact that everyone, including the Islamic countries, knows of this ability, the logical assumption on the part of the world and more importantly on the part of the Moslems would be that the Israelis were responsible for any such strike. This would simply instigate the very war, and its consequences, we are here to prevent. No, I'm afraid we have no other choice but to send one man to do the job, and hope he has the ability to succeed."

The meeting ended with the three men solemnly shaking hands.

It seemed nothing was going well for Michael Bradley. The day that wasn't yet half over was already the most frustrating day of his young career in research. The spectrum he had so carefully prepared using the last of his laboriously synthesized sample was obviously useless. Somehow the KCl pellet he had used had been contaminated with water. The peaks of the jagged infrared absorption trace attributable to the precious manganese complex he had been fighting to study were completely obscured by the familiar peaks of water contamination.

He snubbed his cigarette out in the Petri dish he used as an ashtray, only long training overpowering his desire to rip the spectrum into small pieces. Instead, he carefully added it to the hundreds of other spectrums of the complex, safely bound under a long hard cover, his hand lingering gently for a moment before shoving it violently across the high lab bench.

"You know this isn't the only lab in the country, Mike."

Bradley looked to the source of the voice; a giant man plugging the doorway into the adjacent laboratory. He wore his customary blue plaid Pendleton shirt, draped loosely over his swollen torso and the top of his baggy, blue work pants. His conservative, black shoes seemed ready, as always, to burst with the strain of accumulated weight. Keith Peterson was a brilliant inorganic chemist who had consistently given freely of his time and knowledge while Bradley was courting the secret of how electrons were dumped out of the mechanism of photosynthesis.

"You know, Keith, I still can't believe it. We're so damn close — you know the poloragraphic paper's just been accepted for publication by the Journal of the American Chemical Society?"

"Yeah, I know, Mike." Peterson's career had also suffered from the mysteries of research fund allocation. "Let's get out of here. We've got time for a corned beef sandwich before happy hour at the Steer and Spirits."

"No, Keith. It isn't that simple. I just can't get drunk and forget this one. Doesn't Johnson know what he stands to win?"

"Johnson knows too well what he stands to win. It's what he stands to lose that's bothering him." Bradley's thoughts returned to the morning's group meeting where all his hopes and dreams evaporated in the glow of the silky voiced Johnson. Professor Johnson was known derisively by his group as the "Silver Fox" because of his highly Brylcreemed, silver gray hair and flashy checked, but well-tailored sport coats. Johnson had opened the meeting as he opened every meeting of the group.

He started by flipping open a manila folder of reprints, letters and personal notes with professionally manicured hands. Bradley had once made the mistake of handing Johnson a wet test tube to scrutinize after he had asked about a reactions progress. A quick intake of breath from the other group members present had told Bradley it had been a mistake. A miffed "hmm" was immediately followed by Johnson handing back the test tube and wiping his hand on an instantly produced monogrammed handkerchief. Johnson leaned back, smiling broadly.

"Questions?" The acceptably long silence.

"Problems?" The same long pause.

"Statements?" This was followed by laughter, forced by the group so Johnson would not be laughing alone at his own overused humor.

"Well then, I'd like to start. He asked each member of the research group what progress they had made in the past week and

24

the group discussed the new research and recommended papers they were aware of on the subject. When it came Bradley's turn, the format was changed.

"Mike, before you start I'm afraid I have some bad news." Johnson straightened his tie that was always perfectly aligned rather than meet Bradley eye to eye. "As you know, I've been awaiting word as to the renewal of your grant from the National Science Foundation." His hands shuffled through the papers in the open folder until he found the letter. It was slowly passed hand to hand, down the meeting table to Bradley. "As you also are aware, I've been juggling other grants this past month to keep you working, but now that we know we will be supplied with no further funds for your project at this time . . . I have no choice but to shelve it for awhile." Bradley was skimming the letter, but the meaning was unmistakably clear – "No further support for manganese based release of surplus electrons into water during photosynthesis." It had long been known water was the recipient of these electrons with the corresponding release of oxygen. The question was, "How?" Bradley thought he had the answer. He also believed Johnson thought he had the answer. "Of course, we will be able to find you a new project, Mike."

"I don't need a new project, Professor Johnson, you know that!"

"I'm sorry, Michael, but you must understand I sincerely have no choice in the matter." The finality of the statement was underlined by more paper shuffling and the continuance of the meeting on another topic. Bradley had left the meeting room with his head spinning with pent up anger.

"Come on Mike, you can't stay here today. Let's go somewhere. I'm starving."

"Thanks, Keith, but not today. All right? I just don't feel happy enough for happy hour. OK?"

"Sure, Mike." He started to go but turned back to his friend and sometime collaborator. "Just remember that there are other projects just as good and who knows maybe you'll be able to come back to this one someday."

"Shit, Keith, if we put this down for awhile, we're sure to get scooped. I can't take it anymore. I have to think, but I have a feeling I'm getting out of research. If money is so important, then maybe industry has got the right idea. No grand motives, just do a job and collect a fat salary. You know, nine to five for an oil company or something."

"Quit before you've finished your PhD, Mike? I just can't see you doing that . . . or working for an oil company."

"I don't know . . . I've got to think about it."

"Sure, but don't make a decision that you'll regret later. Sometimes it's hard for us to see what's really happening on the outside. I'll see you tomorrow, OK?"

"Yeah, see you tomorrow."

The afternoons after the weekly group meetings were generally used by the research group as a holiday. This was not surprising as the two or three days prior to the meeting were a frenzy of activity, as each of the group searched for new data or attempted to interpret the old, terrified they'd seem unproductive at the meeting.

Bradley was the last to leave the laboratory, so with a blank mind he routinely checked the apparatus before leaving. It was an unspoken agreement that the last to go would make sure nothing would flood, burn, or explode during the night. On several occasions, Bradley's own experiments had been saved by a conscientious associate. Bradley stood at the door looking into the darkened laboratory, the red power indicator lights of the electrochemical instruments illuminating the pseudo fantasy world he loved with the soft amber of dozing electronics.

He fumbled with his keys as he locked the lab door and the door to the ugly block shaped building that housed so many different laboratories. The building was ugly for a reason; it had been designed with massive walls of reinforced concrete with a flat slab lowered onto the top. In the event of explosion, the building blew up, not outward into the busy university. He left by his usual route, out the side of the building on the fifth floor and down the external stairway to the ground. In the small parking lot below him, almost always empty, was a surprisingly incongruous scene.

Standing almost at attention, next to an exceptionally long black limousine, was a black uniformed chauffer. Bradley wondered if Johnson or some other money conscious professor had gone completely off the deep end and rented the car for some pretentious social occasion. Walking by the car, the driver seemed to be watching him so he nodded an unimpressed greeting.

"Mr. Bradley?" The question stunned him into an open mouthed immobility. "Mr. Bradley, I have a message." The driver walked stiffly up and handed him a small white envelope. Bradley could see the sweat on the man's forehead and neck above his wilting white collar. The typically hot, smoggy glue that passed for late afternoon air in Southern California had had its relentless effect.

"Are you sure you've got the right guy?"

"Positive, sir. Please read the message." Bradley opened one end of the envelope with a key and pulled out the card.

Mr. Bradley,

I would like to speak to you regarding an important career opportunity. My driver is waiting to bring you to my home where we can comfortably discuss the details so important to us both. Please give me a little of your valuable time.

The car proceeded North on Highway 1, along the coast. Michael Bradley smoked cigarettes and enjoyed the view of the Pacific Coast through windows slightly darkened to avoid the inward gaze of sightseers. The stereo system was as gaudy and costly as the rest of the car, but the tapes for the cassette player seemed to mimic his own collection of music. He was rummaging through the numerous selections when the driver spoke to him over the intercom.

"Sir? The second button on the arm rest will drop a small bar; there is also coffee." He dropped an ice cube into the bottom of a cup and poured the coffee on top.

The drive ended in the circular driveway of a gigantic house overlooking a beach that spread serenely at the bottom of a steep sand cliff. When the driver opened the door the setting sun shone brightly into Bradley's face. The driver led him, still partly sightless, to the entrance of the house. At the large double doors, the driver was replaced by a middle aged butler. After leading Bradley to a magnificent library he left him alone but quickly returned with a drink.

"Bushmills, neat, sir."

His favorite drink being brought to him without request solidified his suspicion over the selection of tapes in the limo. They obviously knew his tastes very well and definitely had the advantage because the butler was no more enlightening than the driver had been. Wanting to be in control of his actions in the meeting that seemed imminent now, he sipped the drink and put it down on the coaster the butler had brought with it.

Bradley browsed; the books were a curious mixture of science, human psychology, and political theorizations. He began to wonder who his meeting was to be with, and why. He didn't get to think about it long, for in a few minutes his host made his entrance.

Small in stature, yet not unimpressive. Bald, but not too old. Thin, but not fragile. Dressed impeccably, but not ostentatiously. He walked nimbly up and grasped his hand firmly. "Mr. Bradley, may I call you Mickey?"

"Mike will do just fine, thanks." He didn't want to seem too eager, but he was anxious to know who the hell this guy was that knew that his first name was Mickey. It wasn't on any document he knew of; the family was still touchy about their short history in the United States.

"For convenience, you may call me Samuel. It is my first name, so it won't be so difficult for you when you learn the rest. That is if you decide to come to work with us. Not that I doubt it, of course, but one must be cautious. Now to get down to business, I think to start with . . ."

"Hey, now wait just a God dammed minute. You know every shitin' thing about me, and you won't even tell me your last name. Why must you be cautious? Why do you say 'with you' and not 'for you'? What the hell is this all about anyway? I think I'm entitled to some answers and if I don't start getting some, you can call back that black freak show on wheels and take me home." At this point, he was feeling pretty proud of himself for being able to be his rotten self after the impressive show that this man, Samuel, had given him. To his dismay, the show wasn't over yet.

"You certainly do deserve some explanation, Mike." The butler came in and gave Samuel a drink. He nodded thanks, took a slow drink, and turned to Bradley. "But you're not going to get one . . . not now anyway." Bradley turned to leave, but he was stopped by the continuing voice. "And you won't go, you know, not that you can't, not that the car isn't waiting outside for you, right now. No we aren't

30

going to force you to stay; we don't have to. You have no alternative. You are incapable of deciding in any other way." There was a long pause. All Bradley's weight rested on the ball of his foreword foot. He was enraged, this guy was so sure of himself. "The car is waiting for you outside, Mr. Bradley." His Irish pride had been insulted, so naturally Irish bullheadedness gained control of his motor responses. He slammed the huge doors behind him and they recoiled with a bang into the wall. They stopped half open.

He stormed down the steps two at a time, wanting desperately to go before he changed his mind. He noticed happily the utter confusion reflected in the driver's features. Turning his head back to the house, he saw Samuel standing in the doorway. His face shattered Bradley's elation; it still held the mask of defiant self-assurance that he wore as closely as his tailored silk shirt. The driver closed the door, ran around and got in himself. The engine started up as the intercom came to life. The voice trembled with a hint of bewilderment.

"Yes sir, Mr. Bradley. Where would you like to go?"

Bradley's thoughts pounded a cacophony of confused images then settled into a hum of rationality. The way he figured it he had nothing to lose. Since Samuel knew everything there was to know about him, and he knew absolutely nothing about Samuel, the only information that could pass between them must logically flow in Bradley's direction. By just going back and listening, he might acquire some fact that could be used in his own interest. He had only to gain. *Besides*, he almost said aloud, *it isn't like me to leave a perfectly good drink.*

"Mr. Bradley, would you like me to take you back to the University?" the intercom mocked, unknowingly.

He tried to think of a quick come back, but the well was dry. "No," was all he said, but the chauffeur knew what was meant. Self conscious of their eyes, he tripped on the first step and almost fell on his face. Graciously, Samuel didn't look at him as he walked by, but Bradley's skin crawled when Samuel said, "You didn't finish your drink, Mike."

They returned to the library and the butler was waiting with a new drink in his hand. Bradley accepted it, sat down, and lit a smoke with what he hoped was an imperceptibly shaking hand. Samuel retrieved his topic without missing a beat.

31

"I think to start with we should talk finances. When our job is completed the group's assets will be divided among the members. Although there are many of us, the individual sums should be substantial. Each of us will play the role of guardian to that part of the group's fortune until such a time it is deemed necessary to reassemble those assets for legal defense funds. Your trust will be carefully laundered cash, deposited in this numbered Swiss account." He handed Bradley a small manila envelope. His mind was spinning again and his mouth was very dry. Absent mindedly he reached for his drink, but the envelope occupied his hand. He pushed the drink off the table with his left hand just as his right hand was burned by the unattended cigarette. It fell also.

"Come, Mike, we'll finish talking over a game of pool." As they left the library, Bradley noticed a flurry of activity as two maids began mop-up operations in the area they were evacuating. *Pool has always worked as a tranquilizer for me,* he thought.

"Beer in the game room, Hans," Samuel said to the butler who was supervising the clean up at the time.

While he racked the balls, Samuel continued, "If you are not fortunate enough to survive, nothing, of course, will be sent to that account. Eight ball. Will you break or must I?"

"I think I can handle it," he said quietly. But his mind was screaming — *not fortunate enough to survive?*

The only ball to drop was the eight. He knew it was luck, but it helped him regain some of his composure as he watched Samuel silently re-rack them. The butler came in carrying a tray with two beers. They were still in their bottles, just the way Bradley liked it. He had gotten into the habit of drinking right out of the bottle while living in the desert, where a beer got hot in the time it took to transfer it from bottle to glass.

They spent the rest of the night playing, while Bradley listened and Samuel explained. It turned out that Michael Bradley hadn't even been considered by the organization's computer until a few days before they contacted him. It hadn't thought him suitable until something he did a week before came into its data banks. That action turned out to be the missing piece of his puzzle. The one last piece it needed to draw valid conclusions about his stimulus response pattern.

He had written an article that appeared in the campus underground newspaper, *The Earthworm.* The article was the end result of a drunken discussion about the anarchist's power to evade capture after his revolutionary act. He had broken the subject down into categories: First hours; Use of the city; Use of undeveloped land; etc.

"When that datum," Samuel told them calmly, "was added to the rest: your knowledge of chemistry, your Vietnam record, your former adeptness at long distance running and desert survival, your military marksmanship training, your . . ."

At this point, Bradley interrupted, "Hey look, I haven't run, or shot, or done any of those things for years; I get tired watching a ball game on TV now. I don't know what you need with a superstar with test tubes, but I really don't think I'm your boy." He was beginning to worry about what they expected him to do. *If I survive . . . my God, what could it be?* Bradley frowned.

"We understand your trepidation, Mike, but you will have adequate time to regain your former athletic prowess. I believe it is appropriate to explain a little of what is to be required of you at this time." Samuel then proceeded with a briefing Bradley knew he would never forget.

"After extensive training from some of the best men in the fields of sabotage and related guerilla tactics, you will be air dropped into the target area. Your civilian skydiving experience will be of great value in the time saved in this area of your training . . ." He said the last part almost happily.

God, Bradley thought, *he must know I only did that twice, then stopped because I didn't like the idea of falling out of an airplane.*

". . . Your equipment will need to be very light to allow you to travel fast and possibly far to the target. The target is well guarded electronically, but it is vulnerable, in that for security reasons, it is deficient in manpower. You will find your way to the target — an underground laboratory complex — and penetrate the perimeter. With the laboratory facilities available there, you will create the means for the target's destruction. This is necessarily open ended because we don't know what will be available for your use . . ."

Uncontrolled, his mind began to race. *Benzene, methane, nitric acid, molecular chlorine, silver chloride . . . What else, what else . . .* the structures of the organic synthesis clouded his mind, then rearranged themselves into a feasible synthesis scheme . . . *Sure, given enough time, the proper reagents and equipment common to any lab I could come up with explosives or extremely reactive acids or . . . what am I thinking about . . . this guy's talking crazy and I'm going right along with him. I must be nuts too.*

"I see I have aroused your interest. Good, it will help," Samuel said with a sick grin.

"Help who? Certainly not any people in the lab." Bradley spat the words, more at himself than his host.

"It is a shame, but you must understand that the job would be incomplete without the death of the research staff. They would only move to a more secure location."

"Shit." Bradley's mind filled with the vision of a burning man, stumbling as he tried to cross a narrow road to the rice paddy on the other side.

"Please believe me when I tell you that we act reluctantly, but we are left no alternative. We have known the general direction of their work for some time now, but until recently we believed productive results were beyond the scope of their resources. An unexpected factor has brought us to the conclusions that not only are they capable of results, but they are quite willing to lose those results on an unsuspecting world." Samuel stopped speaking when he saw the disbelief in Bradley's face.

"Just who are they, and what is it they are so eagerly working for?"

"Let us just say a coalition. Yes, a coalition of an old right wing faction in central Europe and certain well to do men in the southeastern Mediterranean area. The object of their research, Mike, is death. Death on a scale hitherto unknown to man. Death so specific it could run rampant in any large city, killing only those people they consider their enemies. There would be no hiding from it, no running away from it, no way to deceive it. Millions would die in their own homes, not ever knowing that they were but a fraction of the whole. A terrible whole that, taken in its entirety, would be the most callous, most merciless, most efficient genocide the world has ever been shameless enough to devise." Samuel's face was beginning to redden. "In comparison, the slaughter of second world war Europe would seem but a compassionately inept trifling. I'm not qualified to explain details, but you will be fully informed before long."

34

"Who do you represent? The FBI, the CIA?"

"No, Mike, we stand for no government."

"Well, who or what do you stand for?"

"That is a very complicated question. To answer it adequately I would be forced into a lengthy oration on history and power politics."

"You had better get started then, hadn't you?"

"Very well. You know, of course, of the United Nations."

"Why didn't you just say you work for the U.N.?"

"Please let me finish before you draw any conclusions. Now as I was saying, you know that the United Nations was the result of a fearful, post-war world. But what you must realize is the idea of a body to solve potentially tragic problems in a peaceful way is far from new.

"After the Napoleonic Wars there was the Concert of Europe. Its function was to prevent the reoccurrence of the war causing problems that had led to those wars. In that respect, it was a success. There were no more Napoleonic Wars. Unfortunately, the Concert of Europe was not up to the causes of World War I. That war punctuated the failure and death of the Concert.

After the First World War the League of Nations was born. The League was supposed to do the same job that the Concert had failed to do. It was thought that with all they had learned from their earlier failure, diplomats could come up with something that was more effective. The League was, as a result, a more highly structured affair. It had more power to act and it was generally thought that, had the League of Nations been in existence prior to the Great War, that war would never have occurred. That was most probably a correct assumption, but unfortunately the First World War was a phenomenon of the past. The League could not cope with a world again converging to war. The Second World War ended Wilson's dream of a world body for peace.

After the Second World War the world again looked to its leaders for a globe free of war. The result was a meeting of the world's diplomats in San Francisco that ushered in the United Nations. How much do you know about the U.N.?"

"Just what I read in the papers."

"Let me tell you a few things you probably don't see in the papers, or if you do, it's too diffuse to understand what is occurring. But first, to get back to your original questions. We stand for life, Mike. We stand for life of the human race as a species. We owe no national allegiances. We owe no allegiance to the United Nations. We are loyal only to each other and the cause of peace."

"And you heroes are going to cure the world and solve the problems that all those politicians couldn't."

"No. No, we have no such illusions. We simply are going to try to buy the world some time." Samuel almost whispered.

"What are you going to buy this time with, good intentions?"

"Nothing as valuable as that. We simply offer our lives." With this revelation the room was thick with silence for long moments. The stillness was broken with Samuel's continued explanation.

"The problem with these organizations was they were all constructed to deal with a world that no longer existed. It was impossible to create a viable organization to meet problems that were unimaginable to the creators. Each of the organizations would have been effective, had it only to deal with the problems that had catalyzed its formation. That was, and still is, a hopeless impossibility.

"Currently the Phoenix that flew from the ashes of the League of Nations is being strangled into impotency by what has commonly become known as 'Bloc Politics.' The United Nations primary role of provider of 'Peace and Security' has been so twisted that one U.N. observer has stated, 'The United Nations contributes about as much to peace as a battleship or an atomic bomb.' Any longer, even a small problem brought before the U.N. is aggravated into a major incident. The U.N. has become just another way to knife one's enemy. When two sides really want to settle a matter, the last place on earth they would go to settle it would be the United Nations."

"Is the Bloc Politics you mentioned what the Russians do to keep us from getting anything done?"

"Well, yes, but it works two ways. Take Korea for instance. The United States Bloc had been preventing the Peoples Republic of China from representation in the U.N. because of entirely selfish reasons. As a protest, the Soviet Union boycotted the Security Council — a move I'm sure they regret. When the North Koreans invaded the South, the United States rushed through a resolution forming a U.N. army to resist the invasion. The resolution was legal by the

United Nations Charter, but the play could have been stopped if all five of the permanent members of the Security Council had been present and voting. You see, by the Charter, all five of the superpowers of the Second World War must be in agreement for the Security Council to act. Then when the Soviets realized their mistake in boycotting the all powerful Security Council and returned, the United States used the majority its Bloc possessed in the General Assembly to push through yet another resolution. This one, called Uniting for Peace ironically enough, gave the General Assembly the right to act on 'peace and security' matters if the veto of one of the super powers kept the Security Council from acting. The unconstitutionality of the resolution has been debated, but the immorality, I think, is obvious. The United States' huge majority has since been deteriorating. It makes one wonder what action she will take when it is completely gone. At any rate, this was a perfect example of a Bloc acting not for the world peace, but for the propagation of its own policies."

"Wait a minute. Are you telling me that the U.S. is the big culprit in all the worlds' problems?"

"No, No. Don't misunderstand me. I just used that series of events as an example. I could have used any one of a hundred instances in which the Soviet Bloc has resorted to the same tactics," Samuel said quickly, "or the Moslem Bloc."

"What we are going to attempt is an avoidance of this handicap. We have formed our own temporary Bloc. An illegality by international law. A Pirate Bloc, dedicated to only one goal. A Bloc that will have a political life of a week at the longest. We will attain our goal or fail, but either way we are doomed men. Those of us who survive our illegal act will probably be tried as international criminals after that week. We only hope we are successful in delaying the world war, the next war shall become." Samuel finished with a frown.

Bradley felt he should tell him how wrong they were; that they were as bad as what they were fighting against. That he would never help. The problem was he was in full agreement. "If what you are telling me is true, I'll give it a try; I agree."

"Mike, you really don't think I would have told you all this before your full agreement do you? Our printout said your decision would be made within seconds of your being informed the method of the laboratory's destruction was to be left completely up to your own abilities." With this, Samuel started for the door of the game room. Bradley followed, silently toying with the connotations of his last statement.

"But that was before you told me it was for a good cause."

"Yes, it was, wasn't it?"

At the front doors, they shook hands. Samuel explained his car would come for Bradley in the morning, and with a mirthless smile, he turned and disappeared back into the house.

When the limousine brought Bradley home that first evening, he got in his old green Ford and drove to the liquor store and the library. He had it in his mind to prove to himself that what Samuel had told him was *just so much bullshit.* He sat at his desk with a six pack of beer and a mountain of reference books, trying to put what he thought useful information into some sort of condensed form. He had filled the better part of a small notebook when he realized his notes were even more cryptic than the hard bounds he had drawn them from. He leaned back in his chair in disgust and grabbed for a cigarette . . . no matches. He got up to ransack his tiny room for some; the small annoyance amplified by greater annoyances. "I must be addressing the problem in the wrong way." Panic, still no matches; he was becoming very animated. "I wonder just who European right wingers and Eastern Mediterranean super rich could find a common hatred for." The answer came all at once, his mouth working independently from his mind. He lunged for a genetics text.

"How the hell could I be so damned stupid?" He rifled through the pages. Then, there it was in black and white. Maybe not the complete answer, but a place to really start. He skimmed the first wordy part that he wasn't interested in, then began to read in earnest.

"... may be symptomatic of Tay-Sachs disease which is due to a recessive gene. Homozygous recessives fail to produce the enzyme hexosaminidase A with the result that a lipid, anglioside GM , accumulates in the brain. Mental and motor deterioration follow rapidly and death occurs by ... A. O'Brien et al. (1971) report success in diagnosing this defect by ..."

Something was pulling at his attention but he was too engrossed to lower his level of concentration.

"... the recessive gene responsible is reported to have a frequency of about 0.015 in the Jewish population of New York City, but not more than approximately 0.00015 in non-Jewish individuals."

Again, his thoughts surfaced through his heavily beer-slurred voice.

"But the Goddamned frequency isn't high enough. Unless they found some way of ..." Just as he grabbed for a virology text, his mind was forced back to reality by the insistent banging on the door. It was Sharon.

"Just who are you talking to in here?" She said as she pushed in to look around. "I thought we were going to a play tonight. You should have been at my apartment three hours ago. I sat there all dressed and ready to go for an hour. You must be out of your mind. Hell, I must be out of mine; I actually believed all that shit you said the other night, 'It's going to be different from now on Share, I'm ready to settle down now Share, I love you Share.' Well, Mickey Boy, this is it. It's all over for real this time. I just can't go on wondering if you really love me." She threw the tickets to the floor as she turned to leave.

"Share, wait." She stopped and turned, her eyes beginning to moisten.

"Well, what is it? I'll listen, but it won't make any difference this time."

"Do you have a match? I'm all out. You know how much I smoke when I study." Bradley watched as a smile fought to overcome her will power.

"You bastard," she laughed and they were in each other's arms.

"Share, I meant it," he said.

"What, that you love me, or that you need a match?"

"Both."

Sharon rummaged through her purse for a match.

"I'll trade you a light for a cigarette."

"You drive a hard bargain, but all right." Bradley lit both, and asked, "Think I could keep the matches for later?" His mind was so preoccupied that he didn't catch on right away when Sharon answered.

"Oh, don't worry, I'll be around later . . . tomorrow's Saturday."

"Mmmm?" He said, wondering if the virology text would help clear the fog from his mind. Sharon was in no mood for him to miss her subtleties.

"Well, shit. You can have the damn matches. I hope you set yourself on fire with them," she said as she stood to go.

He looked at her; his mind finally letting go of the esoteric biological problem. Her words held no meaning for him. He sat down too overcome by uncertainty to answer her. He studied her long, silky black hair that with every minute movement of her head shimmered in the glare of his unshaded desk lamp. He looked deep into her dark eyes as they glowed with the flame of anger. He longed to once again touch her small round bottom that seemed to exist only transiently as her loose dress occasionally pulled tight. He wanted to hold her, to tell her how much he cared. He wanted to find some easy way to tell her he was leaving in the morning.

Sharon noticed his lack of a quick answer, "Mickey, what's wrong. You're . . . you're not . . . *right* tonight."

"Share, I have to tell you something, something very important."

"What is it? Are you going to call it quits for us?" She sat back down.

"No, Share, I'll never do that. It's just that . . . well, I have to go away for awhile."

"Go away? Go away where? Mickey, you have oral exams coming up."

"I'm not going to be here for my orals."

"Mickey!"

"I can't tell you where I'm going, because I really don't know, or know how long I'll be gone, so I want you to have all my things. Sell them, or give them away, or something."

"But, why? I don't understand."

"I can't tell you, Share."

"When?"

"Tomorrow, in the morning."

"You won't tell me why?"

"I can't." There were other reasons Bradley had fallen for Sharon; this was one, her knowing when not to push it.

"OK, I won't ask any more questions." She put out her cigarette, moved very close to him and they kissed. It was the kind of kiss common only to regretful farewells.

They stayed up very late, making love. Afterward, Sharon fell asleep, but Bradley could not. When the morning light brought Sharon from her sleep, he still sat at his small desk.

"I'm going to go now, Share. Here are my car keys, the others are on the hook by the phone." He handed her the keys while she was still in bed.

"Can't I walk you?"

"No, I think it's better this way." He kissed her.

"Mickey, I want you to have this." She took her chain from around her neck; hanging from it was her most prized possession.

"My Mom's Rabbi gave it to her when I was born; it will remind you of me."

He put the Star of David around his neck, said his thanks with another kiss, then left. As he walked, he promised himself that if he ever got back, he would make Sharon his wife. When he got to the street, he could see the black car waiting for him at the bottom of the hill.

At the airport, there was a not so small private jet awaiting the limousine's arrival. As they pulled up there was a brief flurry of activity as the ground crew removed the braking blocks and the pilot fired up his engines. Down the stairs came a man who reminded Bradley of the man in the aspirin commercials. He laughed when he thought how ludicrously appropriate it would be if the man's first words were, "Five of the six doctors surveyed prefer our product." He prepared for a long flight with some public relations man who was ready to quote him statistics.

His first sight impression could not have been further from the truth. Samuel led him up to the man.

"Hello, Joseph," Samuel said.

"Hi, Sam." A sizing-up look at Bradley.

"Mike, this is Professor Barkman. Professor Barkman, Michael Bradley."

"Glad to meet you, Mike. Just call me Joe; all that Professor stuff is in my past now." Barkman was in his late fifties with a thick white mat of curly hair that met a gray beard with white streaks he kept trimmed conservatively short.

"Joe." Bradley gave a nod, then Samuel continued.

"Joseph used to be a Professor of biochemistry at another campus of your undergraduate school. His specialty was molecular genetics. It's been said that he had a plastic model of the 'Alpha Helix' in his lab years before Watson and Crick got their Nobel, but he was too shy to publish."

"Why must every introduction start with that old joke? They looked at the same literature our group had been looking at, but we just didn't see the same thing . . . unfortunately."

"Sorry, Joe, I couldn't resist." Samuel turned back to Bradley. "Joe will explain the biological angle I felt I was not qualified to tell you. And he'll probably tell you some wild story he has been trying to get us to accept for the last few months, also." This brought an unfavorable response from Professor Barkman.

"Listen, Sam, I believe that wild story. I believe it as I have never believed anything before. I feel he has the right to know what he may be up against when he gets to that laboratory."

"I know, Joe, I know." Samuel was strangely subdued. "It's just that we have no choice, even if it is true. I wish there could be some other way but . . ."

"DAMMIT! You're talking about innocent people's lives."

"I'm sorry. There is no alternative."

"Well, he is going to have to decide on his own when he gets there, and I'm not going to send him in completely ignorant."

Bradley was trying to take this all in, put it into some logical order, but it was no use; he just didn't have enough to go on.

"Good luck on your flight . . . er, both of you." Bradley was glad to see he had been remembered. "I'm sorry, we disagree on this, Joe."

"Hey, it's not the first time I didn't agree with the majority."

Bradley liked this guy, Barkman. "I don't usually agree with anyone," he said.

"Come on, Mike, we'll miss our flight." They watched Samuel's car take him away from the plane before turning to get on board.

After the plane was in the air, and on its way to wherever, Joe got up and went to the bar.

"Drink?" We've got beer, but it's not in bottles I'm afraid."

"No thanks, I never drink before a class." Joe Barkman took Bradley's hint, and got right on with his explanation.

44

"Well, yes." He sat down opposite. "You know, of course, that the way we look is determined by a certain set of coded messages handed down to us by our parents. These messages, commonly called inheritance, are . . ."

"Cut the bullshit, Joe. What I want to know is, are they using some offshoot of Tay-Sach's and if they are, how are they getting around the small frequencies characteristic of that syndrome? Virus?" Joe was visibly taken back by Bradley's outburst, and had a hard time finding words.

"Frankly, Mike, I wasn't told you were that fully informed."

"They didn't tell me any specifics; I just put two and two together. It added up that way."

"This should simplify my job quite a bit. I was hoping I wouldn't have to start from the ground up, but I really didn't know what to expect."

"Well?"

"Let me tell you the data as we received it, then we'll discuss the details of how they did it." This sounded like the long way around to Bradley, but he wasn't about to interrupt now that Joe Barkman sounded as if he were going to say something he could really use.

"A year or so ago our intelligence apparatus noticed that many of the third world's most prominent scientists were quietly dropping from view. It was learned through tracing rumors coming from nomadic tribesmen that a top security laboratory had been located somewhere in the Tibesti highlands of Southern Libya. Further investigation by air revealed nothing. This was because, although unknown to us at the time, the laboratory is almost totally subterranean. The small, well camouflaged portion that is above ground was located through infrared photography. To date, our knowledge of the base is limited to that above ground section.

"Since most of the scientists suspected of working in the new lab were bio-genetics oriented, we were able to piece together a theory as to their work. We considered success beyond the scope of their knowledge and technology. Our role of passive observer was rapidly exchanged for the preparations needed to ensure the installation's destruction slightly over a week ago.

"The motivation for our metamorphous to a beast of destruction was a chance observation made by a biologist doing a bird species catalogue in Chad. He had noticed that a certain species of bird was suffering from some unknown viral infection that caused death. Upon follow up he made the startling discovery that only a small, very specific portion of the species population was dying. His published account was, as he stated in his conclusion, one of the most definitive supports for natural selection since Darwin studied his Finches in the Galapagos Islands. Our computer drew other conclusions.

"We had been dreadfully mistaken in our belief that results were beyond those people in the Tibesti highlands. They had been successful in creating some biological means of attacking a specific genetic section of a particular animal species." He stopped to observe Bradley's reaction.

"What you are telling me is that you people already had an extremely structured organization before the discovery of the laboratory. Why? What brought you all together?"

"You are correct, Mike, the laboratory is a problem that did not exist at the time of our organization's birth. Yet it is so intimately intertwined with the problem that spawned our unification that it was necessary to expand our objectives to include the laboratory's destruction.

"You see, Mike, we are dedicated to the prevention of a world war caused by a new Middle Eastern flare up. We had planned to remove those factors that would invariably lead to the involvement of world powers. Specifically, the more potent strategic weaponry each side in the conflict possesses. We have prepared very carefully for the placement of strike forces into the area, under the guise of a United Nations peace keeping force. They were to approach their targets under their U.N. cover, then attack and secure those offensive positions before either side could react.

"Unfortunately, just as the stage is set for the implementation of this plan, the laboratory problem appears. We cannot act on the first objectives without simultaneous action on the lab. If we strike the lab before the other operation, the Arab nations would have to think the Israelis had destroyed it. The result would be the initiation of the war we need to prevent. If we go for the strategic positions before the lab, the Arabs would solve their entire military problem by the blanket genocide of all the Jewish peoples of the world. Hell, even if their virus is only fifty percent effective, it would make a purely conventional war a sure thing for them. What we propose to do now, is to remove all these potentials simultaneously, then appeal to public opinion to save our lives.

"Without the threat of nuclear or biological war in the area, the major powers can keep themselves out of the struggle yet another time. We hope our action prevents a conventional war also, but we depend on the world community to do most of the work in that regard." Joe shook his head and moved to the bar.

"I'm going to have a drink, how about you?"

Bradley stood up and went to the bar, also. "What have you got besides beer?"

"Name it, we've got it. This will be your last chance to drink for awhile. They have quite a program lined up for you, from what I hear."

"Good, I'm going to need it," Bradley said as he lit up a cigarette. "Can I get a Tequila Driver here or do I have to go down the street?" They both laughed as he made Bradley's drink.

"Go easy on that, the tequila in it is a hundred and fifty proof," he cautioned, as Bradley took a more than healthy first swig.

"What the hell, that's only seventy percent, I'm used to drinking ninety-five percent ethanol when I'm in lab, in Orange Crush!"

"I thought you knew something about biochemistry. It's not the ethanol in tequila that gets you, it's the other garbage."

"Oh, yeah? Organics?"

Their conversation degenerated to the relative biochemical merits of different intoxicating beverages as they consumed them. After a few drinks the conversation became forced and Bradley could see that there was something else Joe wanted to say.

"Joe, what is it that I don't know?"

"They don't want me to tell you, Mike. They say it will only make your job that much tougher. They are probably right, but . . . but I think you ought to know."

"Then you better tell me, I guess."

"Let me just give you, as I perceive it, the data you don't have. Then you can think about it what you want. Remember we thought

47

that the lab was doomed to failure until the biologist's report on the death of the birds in Chad. I still think that a discovery of that nature was beyond those people if they were working alone.

"About six months ago, one of my closest friends, a brilliant geneticist with a more than working knowledge of practical virology, was flying with his family over Europe. The flight was reported missing and about fourteen hours later its charred wreckage was found. The bodies were identified by personal objects such as watches, rings, and the like, along with dental records. The doctor and his wife were identified in this manner, but his daughter had to be identified from her personal belongings alone. You see, her dental records could not be located. The thing that struck me as off key was the fact that the doctor and his wife both wore dentures; his daughter did not. By the way, she was a grad student in biology."

"You think that the crash was maneuvered in order to kidnap them?"

"That's the data, draw your own conclusions. It wouldn't have even bothered me, except for the fact that I knew he was getting grant money from the Department of Defense."

"You mean he had already been doing research on that problem."

"Maybe not the same one the people in Libya were working on, but I'm sure it was in a related area."

"Our government didn't do anything about it?"

"If you mean the United States Government, no. They are sure that he died in the plane crash."

"Jesus! Don't they know what's going on in that lab?"

"All indications are that they don't know of the lab's existence. Most of the men that could have brought it to the U.S. Government's attention are part of our organization. As a matter of fact, that is how we first found out about it."

"What did you people do about it?"

"Until the birds died, we did nothing."

"Well, what did you do after they died?"

"We started looking for you."

The pilot came back and told them to prepare to land. As Bradley buckled his seat belt, he looked out of the window. What he saw was very familiar to him, as he had spent a large portion of his life in the Mojave Desert.

The plane landed on a dry lake bed and was met by an old Army Jeep covered with sun baked mud. As Bradley shook Joe's hand in farewell, Barkman suddenly gripped it very hard, looked into his eyes, and spoke in sobering tones.

"One more thing, Mike. The doctor and his family have never been anti-Semitic, but they are not Jewish themselves, they could be perfectly healthy and still be infected. I'm sorry to put this on your shoulders, but it's got to be your decision. It only takes one person to infect the entire world. You *do* understand me?"

"Yes, Joe, I understand you."

Bradley waved as the Jeep took him out onto the lake bed. It wasn't until then that he fully understood that when Joe Barkman had said only one person, he had meant present company included. Bradley realized he too could be a carrier.

S tone didn't have the nerve to turn the radio on as he drove. The Security Council had met in the morning and he had offered his resolution. In an extremely rare show of cooperation and agreement, the resolution had passed on the first vote. The United Nations Mandate in the Middle East was now officially extended. Troops from ten member nations were to be sent in to act as an awesomely threatening deterrent to renewed aggression by either antagonist.

The meeting had been adjourned immediately after the vote. The delegates had all gone their separate ways. Stone was on the road to his home in Connecticut to be with his family when the news broke. He knew he was fortunate in that even if the plan failed, he would expect nothing worse than a ruined reputation and the loss of the only job he knew. Unless, of course, the truth about the conspiracy were to come out prematurely.

Stone wondered what would become of the man he had met only once before the vote. The Soviet system was not as forgiving. The man called Markov could only expect the worst, no matter what action the United States government decided to take.

Stone knew what the probabilities were of that action being just what the Bloc had expected, yet he was still uneasy. He couldn't picture the President of the United States committing American troops into the Middle East region at such short notice, no matter how great the temptation. But he must; the entire program depended on him doing just that. If the Americans honored the U.N. resolution and did send troops, the Soviets would be left no alternative but to send an equally large balancing force. The Chinese would be glad to have helped put the U.S. and Soviets into such a compromised position and would stand by to befriend the alienated third world nations.

Stone pulled into the drive and the front door of the house burst open. He was met half way up the walk by his family. Over the chorus of "Daddy, Daddy," he heard the one question he had known his wife would ask.

"Have you been listening to the news?"

"No . . . no." The group migrated into the house.

"The President has called a news conference. It just started." The television was blaring. Stone caught the tail end of the announcer's filler.

" . . . Sources have gone as far as to intimate that the United States ambassador acted on his own initiative, without prior approval from U.S. policy makers . . ."

"It's been more than intimations, Robert. You should hear what some of the other channels are saying about you."

"I think the President will explain it one way or the other." The President was introduced and when the applause died down, he began to speak.

"Gentlemen of the Press. Oh, excuse me, Ms. Workmen . . . gentlepersons of the press." Laughter welled from the journalists, with an unintelligible reply from a lady reporter, followed by more laughter.

"I called this news conference to place my position on the Stone resolution on record . . ."

"God, no," Stone gasped.

"Although I have not had the opportunity as of yet to speak to the ambassador, I am shortly to do so by telephone. I plan to congratulate him on his perfect timing in introducing our new policy. This policy is designed to remove national barriers for the good of all mankind. Ambassador Stone was instructed sometime ago to be prepared for a day such as this to begin our tremendous task . . ."

Stone stood up and lowered the television.

"I need a drink, Hon. Will you join me in a toast?"

"Of course, Robert, I'll make us some very dry martinis."

"No . . . I feel like some of that good Irish whiskey I brought home last week. Oh, and don't ruin it by mixing it with something, I'll take mine neat." The drinks were made, and Stone offered his happy toast.

"To success!"

"Success!" Stone's wife didn't fully understand, but she had lived with her man long enough to know when he had gained a personal victory. She was pleased. She was far from alone.

The Jeep's engine noise was overwhelming, so communication with the driver was impossible. Bradley decided to take in the sights. The desert is something that one has to get used to before one can fully appreciate its beauty, and he found the surroundings breathtakingly beautiful. As the Jeep raced up the rutted dirt road at, or near, its fantastic top speed of forty-five miles an hour, Bradley tried to place himself. They were definitely moving into an area of much higher elevation, as the creosote and salt bush were giving way to joshua trees and even some small pinyon pines.

Hell, he thought, *we could be almost anywhere, I should have paid more attention during the flight.*

The gradual climbing decreased and stopped. They continued to follow the pitted trail as it wound around rocks and large plants. They crossed a small plateau and began the descent of the much steeper, far side. Bradley stopped counting the switchbacks in the road when the driver nearly failed to negotiate one of the hairpin turns. He held up one hand with his thumb protruding downward; the driver found this very amusing. When he smiled, Bradley saw that his front teeth were caked with a hard layer of mud. It was then that he realized that the trip was going to be more than a quick jaunt across some pretty desert countryside.

When the road funneled out onto another dry lake, the hitherto obvious trail fanned out into scores of random Jeep tracks. The driver added a new set as he drove aimlessly onto the white powdery dust. He pulled on a large, ugly set of goggles and threw Bradley a pair, taking his hands off of the wheel much longer than seemed safe. Bradley finally got his goggles on as the Jeep crossed a cloud of dust it had kicked up on an earlier pass. Too late . . . his eyes were already burning from the alkali suspension. Upon their emergence from the dust, the driver chose an obviously little used dirt road. They drove for another hour, occasionally turning off on an intersecting route.

They had been climbing a steep hill by driving up a soft sand wash bed for a few minutes, when the driver turned out of the wash and took the high ground to the crest of the hill. He slowed down to a fast walking pace and pulled his dirty goggles down around his neck with one hand as he pointed to the valley below with the other.

"Death Valley." The desert swallowed the sound of the engine and the driver's yell, so Bradley leaned toward him to hear better as he took off his goggles. "There is a rock monument down there, some sort of religious sect blazed the first trail across the Valley using covered wagons. I guess a lot of them died. The monument is to them; I'll be damned if I can remember who they were . . . It's a nice monument though, you ought to look at it sometime."

Bradley was about to answer, but when he looked back to the driver he was already fumbling with his goggles. Bradley also pulled his sweat muddied goggles back into place and with a quick acceleration they were again on their way. After crossing the mountain ridge the driver hit him in the arm and then gestured down to an indentation between two Mountains. Bradley tried to wipe the plastic lenses on his sleeve but they were too caked with dirt and he only managed to scratch them. All he could make out were a few dark spots on the tan background. He was unable to tell if they were large Creosote bushes or vehicles. They drew closer and the spots became more discernable — two vehicles, no, one vehicle and a small building.

The building turned out to be a Quonset hut with a dull, brown roof. The vehicle was a mud covered Jeep like their own. They were met at one end of the Quonset hut. The driver shook hands with the man at the door and made a feeble attempt at an introduction.

"This is Bradley," accompanied by a sharp jerk of his head in his direction, "and this is the man you came to see," speaking to Bradley through mud encrusted teeth. They stood silently as the new man spat an overused chew of tobacco onto the powdery desert sand. A wisp of red brown dust rose with its impact. Once his mouth was emptied, he spoke.

"All right, he's delivered. You can take off."

"I'll need a receipt."

"No . . . you don't need a receipt." He turned to go back into the hut. Bradley began to get interested. The driver called after him, an unspoken challenge in his voice.

"I'll need a receipt . . . It's the rules."

It seemed to Bradley that his new acquaintance grew visibly as he straightened his massive torso and turned to the driver. Bradley began to realize for the first time just how awesome an appearance he had; his skin was deeply tanned, with a leathery texture that defied all attempts at guessing his age. Bradley knew he wasn't young, but just how old, he didn't know. He had a bushy, yet well trimmed beard and no hair at all on his head. Bradley could see in the bright sunlight that about half his head was naturally bald, but instead of trying to comb what he had over his pate to make himself look all hair, he had shaved what he did have to look all bald. He wore government issue tan fatigues, but his boots were obviously expensive civilian climbing grade. From his belt hung a black metal bayonet Bradley would learn later was double edged with a blood groove down the middle and a holster supporting a forty-five automatic with a custom competition grip. His eyes must have been blue in his youth, but had since been bleached to an opaque gray by the unforgiving sun of the desert. The gray eyes had a sad look in them that seemed to say, "I'm not fooling, don't push me!"

"Son, out here I make the rules and you don't need a receipt."

A few moments of silence, punctuated by the sound of the corrugated steel roof of the hut groaning in the wind, warned Bradley to expect the worst. He stepped back from the two men, subconsciously betting on the older man. But a fight was not to be, the driver mumbled something to himself then turned, jumped into his Jeep and raced off in a cloud of thick red brown dust. Again silence with only the groaning of the hut.

"Come on in out of the sun, boy, you'll get burnt." The only evidence of the Jeep was the lethargic column of dust climbing gradually up the same incline it had earlier descended. "You see, boy, he's never supposed to take the same way twice, but out there, in his Jeep, *he* makes the rules."

Bradley had realized that the man was at least double his own age, probably more, yet he still wouldn't have run a foot race with him. He followed the older man into the hut, wondering if there was anyone else inside. There wasn't.

The first task the old man gave Bradley was to go out into the desert and bag a jackrabbit. He insisted this was an essential first lesson.

The first day Bradley tried it, he asked how much water he could bring with him. The old man just smiled and asked him how much he thought he could carry. Bradley grabbed the biggest canteen he could find — four quarts. He checked his knife and his hat, made sure his boots were laced and threw the nine-pound jug of water over his shoulder. When he turned toward the door, his trainer flung it open. The eternal dusk of the room was shattered by a white explosion of light. At first Bradley was totally blinded, but as the seconds ticked by, his blindness subsided to one of the most eerie images nature can create. On a field of infinite blackness floated a shimmering rectangle of some viscous, phosphorescing, white fluid. A moment passed before the silhouette of his companion appeared; an almost indistinguishable movement in the glare that was accompanied by his voice.

"You'll need these, boy." Something hit Bradley in the chest then rattled to the concrete floor. He bent down to get his eyes closer to his search. Sunglasses. He put them on as he stood back up.

"What if I just decided that I don't want to go out today?"

"Then I guess you don't go out . . . today."

"Can we just go on to some other part of my training?"

"Nope. This comes first."

"If I can't catch one?"

"I'm a patient man. It's up to you."

"And if I stab you with my knife, steel your keys and drive out of here?"

"Well, boy, if you do that, you wouldn't need a trainer anymore. You'd be ready for whatever you have to do." He stepped out of the doorway into the darkness. Bradley walked out into the sun with the realization that he couldn't have stabbed the man if he had tried. It was the first of many times he noticed the trainer was always in a more superior natural position than any potential enemy. Like a wild cat taking to the high rocks. In this case, he had kept the light behind him and could see Bradley clearly; but Bradley hadn't had the faintest idea where the other man was after he had stepped from the glowing doorway.

He hadn't gone too far before discovering the difference between the abstract concept of a gallon of water and the reality hanging from his shoulder by an unpadded strap. He stopped to redistribute some of the weight from the canteen to his body. While drinking, he tried to think of some tool that could be made to facilitate his opponent's capture. His first thoughts were the ones anyone would probably get, composed of ideas like bow and arrows, slingshots, and traps that use rope lassoes to loop the unsuspecting prey, pulling it upside down when the sapling the rope is tied to springs erect. He realized if he was serious about catching a rabbit, he would have to put these ideas quickly aside because of their inherent infeasibility. He knew it would be foolish to waste time trying to find a sapling in Death Valley.

He decided to hike to the nearest high ground and observe the terrain below. The hike was hot and slow in the loose sand. He was beat by the time he arrived at the rocky hill of his choice. He climbed to what appeared to be the highest point, sat down, and removed his canteen. He thought this was as good a time as any to begin reconditioning his indoor skin, so he removed his shirt and let the bright sun heat up his back. He sat with crossed legs, his hands on his knees, trying to remain perfectly still while he regulated his breathing as he had been taught in Yoga class. Inhale as slowly as possible, count to three, exhale as slowly as possible, count to three, inhale . . . His eyes wandered over the red brown mountains that rimmed the valley for long minutes, then fell slowly to the valley itself.

Lazily, he scanned back and forth across the basin floor, gradually approaching the base of his rocky pedestal. His eyes methodically devoured and sent along to his subconscious the images observed as they traversed and ascended the incline toward his seat. Finished with their half-hour exploration of the surrounding miles, they grew heavy and twitched closed . . . inhale. . . . exhale . . . inhale . . . exhale . . . *arroyo in the mountain opposite is greener than the norm* . . . inhale . . . exhale. *There is a wash in the far east of the basin, flora there is more dense than the rest* . . . inhale . . . exhale. *Rock outcropping below and to the right is not the same color as others nearby* . . . inhale . . . exhale. *The outcropping is white, others near it are red brown* . . . inhale . . . exhale . . . *white outcropping is capped with twigs — NEST* . . . inhale . . . *Eagle? Buzzard? Hawk?* . . . exhale. His eyes opened as he realized the pain that had developed in his legs.

He stood up shakily and then stretched out the stiffness the prolonged sit had caused. After replacing his shirt and canteen, he moved cautiously to his right, looking for the bird's nest. He circled around it slowly so as not to disturb any inhabitants. Occasionally, he stopped to listen hopefully. Baby chicks would be noisy and ready to eat. He wondered if any desert birds of prey fed on jackrabbits. The closer he grew to the mat of twigs, the less hopeful he became. He found the nest had been abandoned. For how long, he couldn't tell — one season, two? In the desert things have a habit of avoiding the logical flow of time. He dropped to one knee and picked through the litter of small white bones surrounding the dilapidated nest. Skulls of the various rodent meals, consumed long before his approach, gave mute testimony to the fact that the past resident had indeed been an efficient hunter. He would not steal his prize, not from this nest at any rate. He carefully placed his behind in the middle of the pile of sticks and let his legs dangle over the edge of the rock. A slight breeze slid warmly up the rocks and through his hair as he again took in the sights of the valley below.

The sun was now far passed its highest point, yet still glared brightly. The ridges on the far side of the basin were already changing color for the night, as shadows moved down their faces. Although the bird's outcropping was not the highest spot on the hill, it was situated in such a way as to give a more unobstructed view of the terrain below. The little white bones he sat on were no accident; the bird had definitely known where to build. Bradley realized that he had a lot to learn, and the best way to learn it would be to give himself entirely to the old man's instruction.

He stood up and started the long walk back to the Quonset hut. The hike wasn't as hot now, but it seemed to be longer. When he arrived the smell of cooking made him aware of how hungry he had become. Inside the old man was frying something on the countertop butane stove. He didn't turn around when he spoke.

"You get one, boy?"

"No, not today."

"Not ever, if you spend all your time sittin' on your ass, playing Kung Fu." He laughed loudly, without turning. Bradley realized he must have followed and watched his progress. Bradley didn't want to talk about his failure, so he tried to change the subject.

"Well, maybe I'll do better next time. What's for dinner?"

"Jackrabbit, boy. Fried jackrabbit. Tastes sort of like fried chicken." He began to laugh again and continued laughing throughout the meal.

"It doesn't taste anything like chicken, tastes more like crow," Bradley joked. They laughed together for the first of many times.

WASHINGTON (AP) — Pentagon sources revealed today that General Silas Riley has been placed in command of the U.S. Army's Fourth Armored Division currently being reassigned to the newly formed United Nations Middle East Deterrent Force (UNMEDF). Military personnel from ten member nations, numbering in the tens of thousands, are at this time traveling to the Middle East where they will take up defensive positions along the demilitarized frontiers of the antagonist nations. Major General Antonio Alvarez, Supreme Commander of the UNMEDF, has stated that his forces would be up to strength within the month. The Spanish Commander explained the U.N. Mandate in this manner:

"United Nations forces will act as a non-passive buffer between opposing armies. The U.N. forces consist of highly mobile armored units that will consider as an enemy, and confront, any unauthorized military intervention into the U.N. buffer zones. Should a major offensive be launched by either side, predesignated naval units of the U.S. and U.S.S.R., now on station in the Mediterranean, would immediately fall under complete U.N. control. These naval forces would provide the UNMEDF with any sea and air support deemed necessary to protect ground operations."

Advance elements of U.S. Fourth Armored Division embarked today from Norfolk, Virginia. Their assumed destination is the Middle East where they will join the UNMEDF . . . .

As Bradley's days at the hut passed, the old man reworked him, both in body and mind. His body grew strong and his skin tanned from extended trips into the desert. Under the close supervision of the old man, his mind became in tune with the life cycles of the other animals of the desert. He no longer had to think about where water could be found, or which places were favorable for hunting; he simply knew. The old man told him in one of his rare gifts of praise, that this intuitive feel for the ecology of the desert was the most important single factor in desert survival. The ability to relate the various animals to their food source not only allowed for their location, and eventual capture, but gave an easy means of distinguishing the edible plants from the poisonous. Bradley's speed in acquiring this feel, he was told, ranked him with the best the old man had ever trained. Before long he was doing many chores for the hut, even catching jackrabbits.

From this point, his training took on what he considered to be the more serious problems at hand. They rose at sunrise and devoted entire mornings to hand-to-hand combat. Bradley was surprised with the speed in which he recovered and surpassed his long forgotten knowledge of karate. The old man was not only a black belt with all the more artistic movements gracefully executed, but had over his many years of practical experience developed an even more devastating, if slightly less aesthetic, symbiotic of the Eastern disciplines and what he called "Awareness of Position." During their first week together, the obvious examples Bradley had noticed were things such as the rarity of him finding himself between the old man and the door, or the fact that Bradley always fell asleep before him, to awaken to the smells of breakfast cooking.

After the morning workouts, they would eat a light lunch and then return to work. Afternoons were devoted to the science of weaponry. Starting with the garrote and bayonet, slowly working through longbows and crossbows, all the way into modern conventional weaponry, both theory and practice. Bradley relearned the mechanics of the world's most common weapons, becoming most adept with the American M-16 and Russian AK-47, yet possessing a working knowledge of any weapon he would likely encounter. When Bradley asked the old man about spending so much time with sniper rifles, he had avoided a straight answer with: "Never know what you're gonna' need to know, boy." Bradley didn't care for the sniper practice, as it reminded him of uncomfortable memories of his tour in Vietnam.

Evenings were for the most part spent in the hut, although occasionally they would go out for some night learning. They went over and over topographical maps and aerial photographs of the area into which he was destined to be air dropped. Four practice jumps were all Bradley had time for, but the old man had declared him "good enough."

In the last days with the old man, aerial films of the target area were dropped to them regularly. Each of those last nights they would put up the slide projector and screen, surveying the day's changes in the lab's outward appearance, measuring the gradual process of a desert reclaiming its own. He learned the landmarks around the secret laboratory's entrance, as the entrance itself had been blended into the terrain almost perfectly. Bradley's final hours before sleep were given to studying a side of chemistry to which he had had little exposure prior to his new life: the practical side of explosives, corrosive agents, poisonous solids; liquids; gasses; and biologically produced toxins. His studies were structured around a sort of mail order specialty course. The old man knew little, and cared less, about this side of the training. He seemed to consider it a waste of time.

It came finally, a complete surprise. One night after a particularly long and detailed session with the maps and photographs of the target area, the area Bradley was at some nebulous point in the future to be parachuted into, the old man leaned his wooden folding chair back on two legs and prodded into his chest pocket with two thick fingers for his chewing tobacco. Bradley realized he had something important to say and being the careful man he was, a short delay to rearrange his thoughts was natural.

"Boy, you're ready as you're gonna' get. We're drivin' out of here in the morning." He stuffed his mouth with the chew then looked to Bradley, waiting for him to speak. Bradley's mind filled with questions that tangled into a confused jumble of disjointed ideas before he could talk. For a long moment, he stared blankly, then his mouth started without first checking with his brain.

"Who's going to take care of the hut?"

"I'll turn on the burglar alarm before we go, boy," the old man chuckled, "and I'll hire a neighbor kid to water the lawn." He laughed so hard he choked on his chew of tobacco. Bradley laughed with him as he beat the old man on his back. Finally his face red and his amusement semi-controlled he stood and crossed to the little refrigerator. It didn't work very well, as the five horsepower gasoline generator that supplied the hut with electricity was timed to start up at dusk and turn off at midnight. But as long as the refrigerator door wasn't opened during the day, it could keep rabbit meat fresh about a week.

"I've been savin' something for just this time," he spoke with mock seriousness as he walked, "Been keepin' it in my footlocker till this afternoon. Put it in the box to get cool right after supper; soon as you started lookin' at those books of yours." Bradley had no idea what he was rambling on about, but he decided to play along.

"It's awfully sweet of you to give me a going away present, but you really shouldn't have put it in to get cold." The old man pulled his head out of the refrigerator, wondering if Bradley knew what he had been hiding for the past six weeks. He had taken the bait, so Bradley yanked him out of the water and onto the boat. "Shit, you should know me well enough by now to realize I prefer my women a little on the warm side." They laughed again as his trainer reached back into the refrigerator.

"My little footlocker couldn't hold a woman boy, but it *was* big enough to hold this." His hand shot up over his head and Bradley saw for the first time what all the excitement was about.

"I'll be damned," he gasped as his mouth became suddenly very wet. The old man held the tattered paper carton by its handle with one hand and supported its bottom lovingly with the palm of his other. The red label, although a little worse for wear, was still legible. Printed in the large familiar script was the holy word, "Coors." He walked slowly to the small wooden table and gently placed his prize in the center of the unfolded topographical map. The caps were ceremoniously removed from two and, as they held them out to each other, the old man proposed a toast.

"To the desert." They tipped up their bottles and gulped them down. It was cold and in the bottle, the way Bradley liked it. He drank happily, ignoring the trickle of the beer dribbling down from his mouth. But when they opened their second bottle, the mood was more subdued. Silently, and slowly, they drank. Bradley didn't know what the old man was thinking about, but his mind was obsessed with one question.

"Yes, but which desert?"

LOURDES, FRANCE (NEA) — Well over a century ago a young girl claimed to have had visions of the Virgin Mary here and the history of this sleepy French village was changed forever. Now it appears that history again turns her brush to Lourdes. Five days ago a family of four made public their story of a heavenly vision.

In a tightly written public statement released by the archbishop of this diocese, the family claimed to have seen the young Christ and that he cured one of their two young boys of acute muscular dystrophy. The family members are presently living in rooms inside the church compound because, according to a church spokesman, of the distance from their home in southern Italy. The statement confirmed that an investigation was progressing with the direct spiritual guidance of the Pope in Rome. No time was specified for the projected completion of the investigation and all indicators point to a long wait for any results . . . the statement released to the press stated that during his appearance the young Savior wore cut off shorts and hiking boots.

The next morning as the sun rose over the valley named after death, the old man and the highly trained saboteur ate their last breakfast of instant eggs and black coffee. They left the table uncleared and brought with them only what they would need on the trip to the rendezvous with the plane: windbreakers, stocking caps, goggles, and one small canteen of water. During the drive through the desert landscape, Bradley felt a sense of loss at leaving it. He understood it. He could, if necessary, survive in this, the least forgiving land in the continental United States. He wondered if he would fare as well in the less harsh, yet immeasurably more complex world where man, not the sun, was king. He thought about the generator at the Quonset hut, starting itself up each evening, giving power to that ridiculous refrigerator in its hopeless battle with the heat of the desert. He wondered how many nights the generator would run before its small fuel tank was as dry as the desert air. And, finally, he wondered how long after the generator was stilled, would that valiant little refrigerator stave off the relentless heat so beyond its power to control. He hoped it would be a long time.

Bradley's reveries ended as they crested the ridge overlooking the dry lakebed sought. As they descended to it, the plane arrived and the old man stopped the Jeep to watch it land. "Looks kind of out of place down there, doesn't it boy?" He nodded toward the small plane. "We stay here until we see two greens and a red." Before Bradley could ask what he meant, a green flare arced into the pale blue sky, followed by another green and finally a red. "That's it, boy."

The old man had fired their first green flare before Bradley realized he was going to answer the signal. He reloaded the flare gun expertly, and fired a second green. He saw Bradley's surprised expression, gave a shrug, and then explained. "A person can't be too careful when it comes to people, now can he?"

Bradley watched a miniature figure begin unloading distance obscured parcels as the old man he had grown to trust and respect maneuvered the Jeep around small mounds of blow sand that had accumulated at the base of the ageless creosote bushes living atop the alluvial fan conterminous to the dry lake. The unloading stopped suddenly, leaving a tiny, dark pile on the parched clay of the lake. With decreasing distance more detail became discernable. A man in camouflage fatigues lay across a small pile of light brown cardboard boxes and khaki green jerry cans; he was on his side, his head propped up on the palm of his fleshy hand, his legs extended comfortably. He rose with a stretch as the Jeep pulled up to the private jet and then bent back down for two of the jerry cans. It was the same driver who had first brought Bradley across the pass leading to the Quonset hut training camp six weeks before. The driver nodded his recognition to Bradley as they passed in opposite directions, but he ignored the old man. Bradley watched as the driver strapped the cans to the Jeep and loaded the boxes.

"Is he going back to the hut?"

"That's right, boy." The old man's voice gained enough volume to ensure the driver's ability to hear. "He's going back to our dirty dishes." The driver threw the last box in the back of the jeep and in an instant the Jeep was throwing dust on the two scurrying men amid the laughter of all three. The Jeep sped out across the dried and cracked silt toward the red hills.

"Yeah, he'll go back, turn everything off, restock food, water, and fuel, then seal the place up for the next time we need it." Bradley had a short, mental glimpse of the driver draining the fuel from the generator and opening the refrigerator door.

The pilot awaited their entry, then closed the short hatch-like door without speaking. He moved forward, shutting the lightweight sliding panel to the cockpit behind him. The "FASTEN SEAT BELTS" sign came on immediately. They strapped themselves to the small couch and as Bradley looked around him, he realized the plane was the same one that had brought him to Death Valley so many thoughts and lessons ago. The takeoff was quick and smooth after the initial steep sprint for altitude.

"You want a beer or something; this rig is loaded." Bradley had unbuckled and stepped to the back side of the bar.

"Well, I could drink a beer now that you mention it — wash down a little of that dust." The old man smiled his acceptance of the driver getting the best of him.

The beer was in bottles, icy cold. Bradley wondered if there had been no time to stock it before his last trip or had he increased sufficiently in importance to merit the trouble this trip. He opened the bottles and handed one to his trainer and friend across the bar.

"Thanks. Come around and sit down. I've got something I want to explain to you." Bradley circled to the front side of the bar to take the stool next to the other man. "Do you remember asking me why we spent so much time on snipping? Well, you were right, boy. We didn't need to spend so much time on it. Not if all you were needed to do was take out the lab in Libya. Shit, boy. The point is I wasn't just training you for that. If I was, you wouldn't have had to learn a lot of the things you did. Now I'm no expert at statistics, but I'm not as ignorant as you may think." Bradley wanted to tell him he didn't think him ignorant at all, but he continued on without a pause.

"You see, boy, they got this thing figured from every angle. They've got the odds figured for any possible foul up." He went behind the bar and pushed a toggle forward on the cabin control panel. A small section of the liquor cabinet swung open, the bottles all snugly strapped down to it. He leaned down and opened the combination lock on the cylindrical safe that had been hidden behind the section of cabinets. He stood back up, holding a large manila envelope. He handed it to Bradley. "Open it." It was sealed, but it opened easily enough. Inside was a bound report. *Betrayal: Minimum Probability 66.67%.*

"In an organization as large as this, somebody is more than likely to get greedy. Maybe for money, maybe for power, but it's better than even money that someone is going to stop working for the Bloc and start working for himself. And just what are we supposed to do about it, sue? No, boy, *we* handle it. We handle it quick and quiet like, within the family."

"So you go out and train yourself an executioner, right?"

"We never plan on using you for assassination; we have other ways of dealing with renegades. But like I said, every angle is covered. The game we're playing has stakes too high not to have all our bases covered. If the time comes that we are left no alternative but to resort to less honorable tactics . . . well then, we'll be ready. Enough of talking about things you probably won't ever be involved in. The only reason you were told about it at all is you're too important to what we're trying to do to have you running around blindly trusting everyone you meet. You have a real job ahead of you, boy. One that we know you *are* going to have to do. If you don't take out that lab, all the rest of us together can't make our plan work. Remember that, boy."

Bradley didn't answer him, he didn't know what to say. The rest of the flight passed with only an occasional word between them. The old man read news magazines and Bradley tried to make some sense out of the report in his possession. It was written in the jargon of a psychologist and was much too full of statistical trends and such for him to get much out of it. By the time the plane was preparing to land, all he knew was someone in the Bloc was going to try to knife the rest of them and it might be his job to stop it. He really didn't think he would be able to do it if the time ever came, and he didn't want to think about it anymore. They were getting enough already, they could find someone else to do their "within the family" killing.

The private jet landed at the same airfield where just a few short weeks before he had casually abandoned all hope of a normal life. He got out of his seat and started for the door, still holding the classified document that he had been reading during the flight. The old man got to the door as he did, but before he made his move to open it, he spoke.

"Listen to me, son, and think about it. We all got our jobs in this. Some are small and others not so small, but all of them have got to be done. My job was giving you some tools you could use in doing your job. I did it as best I could in the time they gave me and I think I did a bang up job of it. But the important thing is I *did* it. Now you got your job to do and I know you'll give it all you have in ya. I want you to believe me when I say you can do it. Damn boy? You and me are gonna' sit in some little beer bar some day and bullshit about old times. This ain't the end of us to chasin' Jacks, it's just sort of a delay. You know what I mean?" Bradley had lived alone with this leathery old man long enough to know that he had something on his mind and was just working himself up to it. He knew if he just kept quiet the old man would get to it in his own time.

"Well, what I'm trying to tell you is, they can ask us for more. They can come up to me next week and tell me you got yourself killed, and they got themselves a new boy for me to teach. Now I wouldn't like that, no I wouldn't like that at all. But Goddamned if I wouldn't go right back out to that valley and train them a new boy." Now Bradley saw where he was going with his oblique ramblings. He tried to interrupt, but the old guy wouldn't have any of it.

"Now I ain't through yet and you just listen for awhile. My point is, if after you get back from where they're sending you this time, they come up to you and tell you they need your services for somethin' else . . . Well you're gonna' just say, 'Yes sir, what can I do for ya.' No questions asked. You know. If they come up to you and tell you that someone is trying to steal all the marbles and they want you to fix it so he don't even play anymore, you're just gonna' do it. You see, boy, they need you; they have from the start. You're not gonna' like doing it, no one does, but you'll do it just the same. You ain't got any more choice in the matter than anyone else. They ask and we do, that's the way it is in this thing. They just know who to ask is all." His voice trailed off at the end of his sentence as he threw the bolt of the door and pushed it open.

Bradley began to move toward the steps that led outside but the old man stopped him, a suspicious look in his eyes. "You ain't thinkin' of taken that with ya are ya?" Looking down at the report Bradley held in both hands.

"Uh, no," Bradley answered as he handed him the report, the title staring blankly back at him. A 66.67% chance is a pretty sure bet and the thought of it made his stomach suddenly very light. Bradley started down the steps still wondering about the overwhelming probability of betrayal.

"See you soon, boy. Remember what I said," the old man called after him. Bradley waved his farewell and turned his eyes to the runway.

There shining in the midday sun was the limo, the chauffeur stood by the open passenger's door and inside sat Samuel. He got in next to him, the driver closing the door behind him.

"I've got some questions for you, Samuel," he tried to put all his questions into the meaning of that first statement. Samuel knew what Bradley was asking him, but he wanted him to come right out into the open with words.

"That's why I am here today, Mike," he said as the car got under way. He smiled condescendingly and Bradley blew his top.

"What the hell is all this assassination bullshit? We didn't talk about that before and by God I'm not going to have any part of it. Come to think of it, this whole thing just isn't in my line." Samuel shifted his weight in the seat uncomfortably and Bradley knew he was getting to him for the first time. He pressed his advantage. "Look, I got into this before I had a chance to give it the proper thought. I may have acted to hastily." He looked at Samuel, his eyes demanding an immediate reply. He sat up straight, tugged at his sports jacket, then smoothed some wrinkles from the crease in his slacks. Bradley's thoughts were thrown back to their first meeting. He remembered how relaxed and sure of himself Samuel had been then, and suddenly he was again.

"Well, Mike, I knew that you would take this new development hard, but I had no idea that your doubts would flow over into our previous agreement. Even I was taken completely by surprise by that one." He paused politely for Bradley's answer. He didn't have one at the moment.

"Let me try to explain. The dual nature of your training was purely for practical reasons. It was simply more efficient to give you all conceivably necessary training during one program. Whether or not you ever use all the facets of that training will, of course, be decided prior to the event . . . by you. The time saved, if you ever do decide to help us with some other task, at some future date, is enormous. I can only hope that this small error on my part does not destroy your resolve to perform the mission we agreed on before your training." Bradley knew if he was going to ever back out, this was the time.

"You see, the wheels have irreversibly begun to turn. During your absence a great many people have committed themselves on my word that you will succeed in removing the laboratory variable. We have managed to secure an extended United Nations mandate in the Middle East without raising undue international suspicions. Thousands of troops from a score of nations, the overwhelming majority of these troops Bloc sympathizers, have been sent into the theater. Bloc strike forces at this moment are organized in staging areas. The neutralization strikes are to occur in just a few days. We have no time to train another man, even if there was another with your qualifications. We are now driving to a military airfield where a C-5A transport stands waiting, its engines warming, for its last and most important cargo, you!"

Bradley had not been aware of any of this until that moment and he had been totally engrossed in Samuel's monologue as it brought him up to date. When he finished, it took a conscious effort on Bradley's part to lift his open jaw from his chest. Samuel waited for him to regain his self composure and speak. What he said surprised them both.

"I have no weapons."

Samuel replied with amazing speed, considering Bradley's unexpected statement. "All you will need is already on the transport. The only thing that needs to be added is you."

"I want to make a phone call."

"Really, Mike, there is no time."

"Well, make time God damn it. This may be the last chance I'll get." Samuel gave him a slow thoughtful look, then turned to the intercom.

"Johnson, find a phone booth."

"Immediately, sir." The driver responded emotionlessly.

"I hope you have a pocket full of nickels, this will be long distance," he told Samuel, hoping he did.

"I think we'll manage, Mike." They arrived at a phone booth and Samuel had the charges transferred to his credit card account. Bradley had the operator ring Sharon's apartment. It rang half a dozen times and just as the operator was telling him, "Your number does not answer," someone did. It was a man's voice.

"Hello, is Sharon there?"

"Who? No. Nobody by that name lives here."

"Oh, no . . . well I guess I got the wrong number. Thanks. Bye." They hung up and Bradley had the operator look up Sharon's parents' number in San Francisco. He tried that, but he couldn't understand Share living with her parents again.

"Hello?" He knew it wasn't Sharon, maybe her Mom.

"Hello, I'm a friend of Sharon's from school and I just called her old apartment and found out that . . . ."

He was interrupted by a very excited, almost panicked, outburst, "OH! Is this Mickey? Oh God, Sharon's not here. I mean . . ."

Bradley's turn to interrupt.

"Look, Mrs. Klein, I don't have very much time." Samuel was standing outside of the booth pointing at his watch. Bradley turned away from him and continued. "Do you have a number where she can be reached?"

"No, since she came back, all she does is check the mail, looking for word from you . . . and she takes walks. She is out on one of her walks right now. Sometimes she doesn't come home for hours. Oh, she will be so disappointed . . ."

"Just a second, I'll be right back." Bradley put the phone down and opened the booth door. "Samuel, when will I get my next shot at a phone? I can't get my party."

"What next chance? This was it. You're flying out of the country ten minutes ago!"

"I don't go for the lab without completing this call."

"There *may* be a phone at the other end," he said hesitantly. "That would be about fifteen hours or so from now."

"OK, good enough." Bradley got back to the phone. "Hello, the next chance I'll have to call will be in about fifteen hours from now. That will be early tomorrow morning. Let's say if I don't call by six in the morning I couldn't call, but have her stay home tonight. All right?"

"Yes! Nothing short of a fire will get her out of the house tonight after I tell her you called."

"Fine. Now one more thing, I want you to tell her that no matter what happens — I love her and I'm going to come back to her and . . ." Samuel pointed to his watch again, his face contorted from his anxiety to get going. "Well just tell her I love her and to stay home tonight. OK?"

"But . . . alright, I'll be sure to tell her. Good-bye, Mickey. Sharon will be home. Bye." Bradley hung up and accompanied Samuel back into the car. After they started moving again Samuel sighed.

"Obviously you don't know what a C-5A is.

"I really couldn't care less."

The C-5A was the largest airplane Bradley had ever seen. They drove up to where it sat at the end of the runway, blocking all incoming and outgoing traffic, ran out to it and were met by a member of the flight crew. He ran with them the rest of the way to show Bradley the route to the hatchway. As they drew closer, its engines, that had been loud before, suddenly became unbearably loud as the pilot revved them up. A quick handshake with Samuel, then Bradley was on board. The crew member pushed him into a seat and buckled him in as the plane began to move. The giant plane was off the ground less than a minute after the car had pulled up to it. The crew member had not had time to do anything but crouch down next to, and hold onto, Bradley's seat. Once off the ground he turned to Bradley as he stood up. A big smile filled his face.

"I'm glad you decided to join us Mr. Bradley. You just won me fifty bucks." Then he was climbing the steep incline toward the nose of the ascending plane.

After about an hour the crewman came back to his seat. Bradley didn't notice him at first as the steady drone of the aircraft had lulled him into a fitful, half sleep. His mind was swimming with thoughts, and sometimes dreams, of the events of the past month and a half.

He couldn't find a satisfactory way to fit those events into any logical order. They seemed to float as mist, obstinately refusing to be confined. He would doze, carefully placing them as books on a shelf, almost grasping the magic formula that would bring his life back into understanding, only to drift back awake realizing that some of the events he had been filing away were only the products of his twilight sleep. And the perfect order of a moment before would become mass confusion with a waking start. He tried to think of Sharon and what it would be like for him upon his return. He planned a quick, immediate-family-only marriage followed by an escape to some lonely beach bungalow or mountain cabin. He tried desperately to find something, anything that he could plan, some small thing that could be decided by him, an implication that his life was in fact being controlled by him. The question that haunted his reveries suddenly came into blinding clarity, "Why am I doing this — why am I here?" He had no answer.

"Sir? Mr. Bradley?" The crewman shattered his thoughts with his muted, yet surprising call. Bradley jerked erect and rebounded off the seat belt he had never bothered to remove. He fumbled with the buckle as the crewman continued. "Sorry to disturb you, but I wasn't sure when you wanted to look over your equipment. I wasn't told how long it would take you to prepare."

"That's OK, I don't really know either, so I guess *now* is a good time to start." The crewman motioned him to follow. They walked among gigantic canvas covered forms and wooden crates. He stopped at a crate that was a good six feet square and was marked only, "THIS SIDE UP." It looked very much like the others to Bradley, except the side facing him was hinged at one edge and padlocked at the other.

"This is the one." He produced a key and shortly was dragging open the large square door. Inside looked more like a small room than a big wooden box. The walls were hung with various articles of fatigue clothing, survival equipment and weapons. In the center of the wooden room, secured to the floor, was a large footlocker marked "EXPLOSIVES," taped on the top was a sealed manila envelope with "BRADLEY" written in block letters an inch high.

"I have been instructed to leave you alone here. If you need anything from me, I'll be forward." He turned on a heel and was gone.

Bradley ran a quick eyeball inventory, there was more here than five men could use. He peeled the envelope from the footlocker and tore it open. Inside was a typewritten report with no title. Penciled across the top margin of the first page was a note from the old man, "Remember how heavy things can get in the desert, boy, don't get greedy." The report contained a detailed list of the equipment in the box; all of it was familiar to Bradley from long hours spent at the hut in the valley. He checked off each item on the list as he found them; going over the workings of each instrument slowly to find the weapons that felt best to him. The only tool he was sure of from the start was a knife, the very same type the old man had always kept at his waist.

Gradually, through a process of elimination, the number of possible choices dwindled. Each time he went through the pile, one or two items would be deemed unacceptable for no explainable reason. When he got down to about twice as much as he could carry, he began tearing things down and putting them back together. One item at a time would be placed into one of three piles; yes, no, maybe. Nice watch, yes. Fine four quart canteen, no. Perfect forty-five caliber service pistol, maybe. And so it went. Bradley got out of his civilian clothes, article by article, except the boots he had broken-in during his training. Old Levis were shucked for a pair of paratrooper fatigue pants with numerous pockets and tossed into the corner with the rest of his cast offs.

At last he stepped out of the box fully clothed with his knife at his hip. He looked back at the small pile that had survived the final cut. He knew it was still too much to carry, but he couldn't see how to delete anything else. He was standing, scratching his chin stubble, when the crewman came back.

"I happen to know you haven't had anything to eat in seven hours. How about some coffee and sandwiches?" He was looking Bradley up and down with new interest as he held out a white paper carton.

"Not exactly a wedding tux," Bradley said, pulling out on both pant legs, "but suitable to the occasion at hand." For the first time he realized how hungry he had become. "Yeah, I could go for about ten sandwiches, but no coffee, I'm going to try to get some sleep. Anything else to drink on board?"

"Only about five hundred cases of Hawaiian Punch." He smiled.

"Fine I promise not to drink it all." The crewman broke open a box of soft drinks and doled out some cans. The first use of Bradley's new knife was as a can opener. They ate together, sitting on a crate opposite the one full of equipment.

"I'm gonna' have to close that thing back up before we land."

"How long till then?"

"Another eight or nine hours yet, we'll be landing there at about noon or so."

"Well, I'm going to try to sleep," Bradley said as he crumpled his trash and smashed it into the cardboard box. "Why don't you wake me up about an hour before we land? I'll grab what I need and help you lock it up, OK?"

"Sure, you're the boss." Bradley looked over at him and realized he wasn't joking.

The rest of the trip was spent back at his seat trying to sleep. He finally dropped off after two or three hours of what almost qualified as tossing and turning in the sitting position.

When the crewman woke him, he decided to take every item of his "final cut" pile and discard what he felt was too heavy before the actual hike. The crewman helped him move the stuff out of the crate and Bradley helped him close it up. He figured out what pockets would hold which items during the last hour, placing them with care; lightest at his calves and growing more heavy toward his waist. By the time the transport readied for landing, he was armed well enough to wage what war was necessary. He smiled when he thought of the cartoon so popular in Vietnam. Below a characterture of a Marine ridiculously overloaded with weapons, the caption read, "Though I walk through the Valley of Death I will fear no evil; because I'm the meanest Mutha' in the Valley."

When on the ground, yet still travelling very close to air speed, the crewman, who had sat out the landing beside him, stood up and readied himself by the hatch. The hatch was open before the plane came to a full halt. He jumped to the ground first with Bradley following close behind. He pointed to a small helicopter gunship that was landing thirty yards away, then grabbed Bradley's right hand in his. He stared at Bradley's face with a look that compelled him to remove his dark glasses. They looked at each other for a moment with a strange, silent rapport, the din from the huge jet and the gunship preventing casual conversation, then he leaned close to Bradley's ear and yelled.

"Good Luck! See you in court!"

The last comment made Bradley wonder how much he knew about what he was going to do. Bradley didn't feel much like screaming over the noise, so he just nodded and ran toward the helicopter. The pilot looked oddly mechanical in his bulky head gear as he pointed to the open door on the side of the ship.

Bradley's hand was shook again when he climbed on board. The craft rose to thirty or forty feet, leveled off and made for a group of buildings in a distant corner of the immense concrete-paved airfield. They arrived in front of the main building of the complex, landing in the shadow of the control tower. The crewman who had shaken his hand moved to the doorway and jumped the last three feet to the ground. Bradley jumped also, not knowing where he was going. They ran to the door and passed through into semi-quiet.

There were half a dozen clerks and aviators in a large office-like room. Twice as many desks were arranged in rows. They walked briskly between them, all eyes on Bradley. He wondered why, if everyone was in such a big rush, he was being led into a labyrinth of military paper pushers. They went through a door-less doorway, and started down a well waxed corridor. Various rooms lay on either side, plastic name plates hanging from the corridor ceiling adjacent to each: Briefing Room; HQ 203 Transport Grp; Receiving; Officer Of The Day; General Walker. They turned into the last one, walked passed an outer office and into a walnut paneled inner office. A small fat man with curly hair and a five o'clock shadow stood up.

"My name is Walker." He leaned over the desk, his belly dragging across it, his hand extended. They shook hands.

"I'm Bradley."

"Damn it, don't you think I know that?" He pointed to the phone.

"Line one is open to a stateside operator. New York, I think. You've got fifteen minutes." He looked violently at his watch, then stomped out of the room and Bradley was alone. He didn't remember Sharon's parents' number, so it took 10 minutes and two more operators to get through. Finally, he heard a faint ringing on a phone ten thousand miles away.

"Hello, Mickey?"

"Yes, it's me, Share."

"I can't hear you, what's wrong? Where are you?"

"Far away, but thinking about you."

"Mickey, I have all your things in my parents' garage. When are you coming? I've been so worried." At this point, Sharon broke down, she continued to try to speak, but her words were muffled with sobs.

"Share, Share? We don't have much time . . . Please listen to me." Her sobbing tore at his heart.

"Yes, Mickey . . . I'm sorry." He could picture her as she regained control, her eyes burning with the inner strength he loved.

"Look, Share, my parents don't know anything about this, could you get hold of them for me?"

"I already have, they're worried too." Her voice was very calm now. "I figured you hadn't had time, they're OK, but very confused . . . And so am I."

"Take care of them for me, will ya?"

"Of course, Mickey, what do you take me for?" He was glad to hear her mad.

"Anything I can, babe. Listen if you don't hear from me in about two weeks, I've run off with some barmaid, never to return." He tried to let her know with his tone that it was a little more than a joke.

"Well Goddamn, you know I won't let you off my leash that easily. I'll come and pull you out of any bed in the world, you deviate!" They laughed for a moment, then a loud silence punctuated by long distance hiss filled the receiver.

"Share, I love you and I'm going to do my best to come home to you . . . if you want?"

"Want? Are you crazy? I love you, too, you dumb Irishman. Come back soon."

The fat General came back into the room; he motioned impatiently toward his watch.

"I've got to go now, Share."

"Oh, Mickey? I . . . I love you."

"Me, too. Two weeks maybe, huh." Oh God. She was crying again, and his insides did a flip.

"Share, wait a minute, I . . ." The fat General stuck one fat finger down on the receiver switch and the connection was broken.

At first, Bradley didn't comprehend what had happened; he just stood looking at the phone with the stubby finger, white around the cuticle, jammed down on it. Then the General growled, "Come on, Bradley, you've had more than your fifteen minutes."

These strangers had taken him from the controlled environment of the womb of the University, told him things he didn't understand about politics he hadn't really followed, implied he couldn't make a free choice on any matter they happened to shove at him, burnt him raw in the sun, ran him ragged getting into the best shape of his life, retaught him how to kill with everything from bare hands to rocket launchers, flew him over half the world, told him he was to be an assassin, armed him to the teeth, and were preparing to drop him all alone into desert country he didn't know so he could single handedly attack an underground fortress, where, if he wasn't killed himself, he was supposed to slaughter every human being. And now this paunchy little man had prevented him from telling the girl he loved he probably wasn't ever coming back to her.

He removed his finger; Bradley's eyes followed it to where he finally rested it on his hip. Bradley looked to his face and back to his hand. The General self-consciously took his hands from his hips and shoved them into his trouser pockets as he walked around to the other side of the metal desk.

"Uh . . . Sorry Bradley. But, uh, we're on a very tight schedule around here."

Bradley dove over the desk head first, arms fully extended. The fat man didn't have a chance to move; Bradley's hands hit him in the throat while his body was still horizontal over the desk. They both crashed to the floor as the General let out a terrified scream. Bradley tightened his hold of the fat throat and no more scream. He continued to struggle and punch feebly at Bradley's stomach. It was taking too long, Bradley reached for his blade. He knew just the spot on the man's fat neck where the knife would do the fastest job, the jugular. Then there were men all around them pulling at Bradley's arms and legs. He gave up on the fat guy, turning on the assailants, kicking, punching and flicking his blade. They grabbed the General and backed away. Bradley stood in the corner of the office, watching them as they watched him. His body was trembling uncontrollably. The General was clutching his throat and fighting for each breath. The other men in the room all had a remarkably similar look of confused terror. One man held a profusely bleeding forearm with his other hand. The voice that came from Bradley's mouth was unfamiliar even to him.

"You've got fifteen minutes to get that connection back." He sheathed the knife, pulled the service forty-five from its holster and aimed it at the General, letting the slide slam home. The terrified General's eyes got even bigger than when he was being strangled. He pushed one of the men toward the phone. Sharon was back on the line in ten minutes, the operator had already been working on the disconnection.

"Mickey, we were disconnected, but the operator said you had hung up."

"Sharon, I'll be coming home in two weeks, you be ready to go away with me."

"What's wrong, you sound terrible? What happened?"

"Never mind. I'll see you in two weeks. Good bye."

"What? Mickey?"

"I said good bye." His voice carried a serrated edge.

"Goodbye . . . I'll be ready."

"All right, see you soon."

"I love you, Mickey."

"Goodbye." He hung up the phone and holstered the pistol.

"All right, I'm ready to go now." No one moved, so Bradley started forward toward the door at their backs. He found himself laughing hysterically when they all tried to get through the door at once. He was still laughing when he got back aboard the chopper.

This time, as Bradley pulled the intercom headset onto his head, the helicopter rose high into the air. The view was fantastic, the deep blue of the Mediterranean came rolling over the horizon toward them and then there was only water. Bradley moved forward to the pilot and screamed, "Where are we headed?"

"Out to the Fleet . . . carrier." Bradley was relieved to know that they weren't taking him directly into the target area, but he really wasn't ready for another confrontation like the one he had just left. He still couldn't rationalize his actions. It would have been just as efficient and much less insane simply to refuse to move without finishing the call. He forced the painful thoughts out of his mind.

"How long until we get there?"

The pilot looked at his watch, then called back "'bout forty minutes yet."

"Thanks a lot," Bradley said, putting his hand on the pilot's shoulder as he started to move back out of the way.

"Hey, buddy!" The pilot called after him, so he leaned back forward.

"Yeah, what's up?"

"You don't look nuts to me. What the hell did you pull down there anyway? They radioed right after we took off that you had gone berserk."

He tried to laugh the comment off, but the pilot's eyes still looked wary.

"I don't know. This fat General started treating me pretty badly and I blew up. Tried to strangle the little son of a bitch." The pilot's eyes wrinkled into a smile, then he burst into incredulous laughter. Bradley watched as he tried to stop. Finally, after taking a huge breath, still holding his side, he called over the engine noise.

"I know about ten thousand guys that would'a given a month's pay to see that . . . is he dead?" He was still smiling. Bradley couldn't believe it.

"No, they pulled me off."

"Too bad." Then he broke up again. Bradley really didn't find it that funny, so he climbed back from where he came.

The rest of the flight passed slowly, yet finally they passed over an aircraft carrier and her surrounding support vessels. Bradley had never been on a carrier, he was anxious to get on board.

After landing he was met and motioned to follow. Once he cleared the rotor blades he turned back to the gunship. He was just in time to see the pilot wave to him. He waved back thinking the guy was as nuts as he was. The helicopter lifted and sped off.

Bradley turned to the man who had met him; he held a hand gun. Two men came up from behind and took his pistol and knife. Bradley thought it ridiculous when he remembered pockets jammed full of such delicacies as hand grenades and a dismembered machine gun. They walked toward the tall part of the ship towering over the flight deck. It was sprouted with some large guns, lots of mysterious antennae, and way up on top, snapping in the sea wind, was a red flag with the familiar yellow hammer and sickle. It was only then that the odd uniforms registered in Bradley's mind. It was going to be hard to explain this one, he didn't speak any Russian. They showed him through the maze-like metal corridors to the bridge. The man he realized to be captain dismissed them with a gesture.

"Well, Bradley. So you have already begun to fight! Good, good!" He had a heavy accent, but his English was the best surprise Bradley had ever had.

"Come Bradley, let us drink coffee and talk in my quarters." He spoke in Russian to another officer then turned and walked out, with Bradley following after. His quarters were much smaller than Bradley had expected. A bed dominated the far corner. Book cases lined the two walls above the bed. They couldn't have held one more pamphlet. Each shelf had the normal row of upright volumes, but in addition the spaces between the neat rows and the shelves above were stuffed to overflowing with books that jutted out at all possible angles. A desk, bureau, closet, and a huge overstuffed, black leather chair comprised the rest of the furnishings. He noticed Bradley staring at the chair that seemed so out of place in this small barren room.

"Yes, the chair does seem a bit out of place here, doesn't it? Yet it is very comfortable, I sleep in it often." He smiled then extended his hand toward it, palm up. "Please sit down." He pulled a swivel chair from the desk and sat in it. Bradley fell thankfully into the massive leather chair, it was very comfortable. Someone knocked on the door and a short exchange in Russian followed. It was a man with coffee. He brought the tray in, placed it on the captain's desk, and then retreated from the cabin. As the captain poured he said, "There are sandwiches also, are you hungry?"

"I could do with one, yes." Bradley ate two of the beef sandwiches as they talked.

"You attacked a General. A soldier in my country would be in very grave trouble if he did such a thing."

"I am no longer a soldier. I am a . . . student." The ice on Bradley's last word surprised even himself.

"Oh? I had assumed you to be in the military." He didn't approve.

"I don't understand either, but they seemed to know what they were doing."

"Yes?" He wasn't convinced. "The idea of a secret mission by one man was resisted by me . . . And others." He added the last as an afterthought. "I have little faith that it can succeed. The vessel you are aboard is quite capable of launching successful air strikes on the target. She will most probably be required to do so anyway, so . . ." He saw the effect his casual discussion of Bradley's failure and consequent death was having. "I am sorry, I should not have brought the matter up. It is not your worry."

"I'll do my best to succeed . . . And survive." Bradley listened to his own voice, almost as a third person eavesdropping.

"Of course, and you shall. Now for more immediate matters, I will give you your final briefing later in the day. We have some recent photographs of the area. You will dine with my officers tonight, then be flown to your objective. Leaving the ship in . . ." He looked at his watch. "In seven hours thirty-five minutes. You will arrive shortly after the moon rises." Bradley nodded his understanding. "Until then, you have the freedom of the ship . . . But do not attack anyone here." He had become very, very serious.

"I think I would just like to relax alone somewhere, if you can arrange it?"

"Of course. You can stay here. There are a few books in English on the shelf . . ." He looked to his bookcase. "If you can find them." He was more relaxed now that he knew Bradley planned to stay out of trouble and this showed in his smile.

"I leave you now. I will return to take you to our briefing room in two or three hours." He stood and left without another word. Bradley rummaged through his books and finally found one in English; Lewis Carroll's *Alice's Adventures in Wonderland*. Somehow it seemed to fit. He started at the beginning again.

The briefing room on the Soviet aircraft carrier was very modern, yet somehow alien, as if even the metal of the bulkheads could attest to the fact that Bradley was aboard a ship designed by Russians, built by Russians, and manned by Russians. The captain showed aerial photographs of the target area that had been taken earlier in the day. It was the same area Bradley had grown accustomed to studying with the old man back at the hut in Death Valley. But now all trace of the laboratory, all vehicle tracks, and all dislocated vegetation had been concealed under the mask of the surrounding environment. They went over the area repeatedly using a flashlight pointer that projected a red arrow onto the screen. Bradley memorized relative heights and distances of the major landmarks. Photographs and maps of the jump area, and others of the terrain separating his expected landing point from the target area were compared. Special attention was paid to the target itself. Bradley was convinced that if he wasn't parachuted too far from the expected landing point, he would be able to find the way to the laboratory from memory. As he poured over the maps, deciding which ones he would take with him, the captain switched topics.

"You will need explosives, Bradley, I can supply you with any you think you will need." The doubt was not in his voice anymore. He still didn't believe Bradley could succeed, but he was not going to overlook anything he could do to make his chances better.

"I think I have everything I will need . . . or everything I can carry anyway. Except . . ."

"Oh yes, I almost forgot." He produced the knife and handgun from a box under the table where they sat. "It was a necessary precaution to protect ourselves. I was told you had gone insane." He pushed them across the table top with a smile.

"Well that much is true, the question is, when?" The Russian was slow in understanding, then he laughed deeply.

"Yes, it is an insane thing we do, isn't it?" They laughed together. Bradley picked up the knife he had wanted returned but left the bulky service pistol on the table. "You keep that, it's much too heavy for me to take. I'll leave the holster in your quarters." The captain was obviously pleased.

He picked up the gun again with renewed interest now that it belonged to him. Balancing it in the palm of his hand, he said, "I will use it only against our common enemies, Bradley. Whoever that may be at the time, eh?" He bent down and reached into the box again. When his hands reappeared, they contained a large sealed envelope. "This arrived by air three days ago, more instructions, I suppose." He handed it to Bradley.

On the front of the envelope was typed, "TO BE GIVEN TO MICHAEL BRADLEY PRIOR TO HIS DEPARTURE — SECRET," and below that in Russian what Bradley assumed was a translation. When he looked up, the captain was at the door.

"I shall return in one hour, if you need more time, tell me when I return."

Bradley opened the envelope with his two edged knife. Inside was a letter from Dr. Joseph Barkman and some computer printouts.

Mike,

If you will remember our conversation during your plane flight to the desert training area, you will recall my contention that innocent people were being forced to do research in the field of genetics we discussed. As you know, all the members of our organization I approached with my beliefs vehemently denied their validity. Well . . . I am a very stubborn man when I believe I am right. After our last meeting, I ceased my fruitless efforts to prove my ideas, not because I doubted them, but because I began to feel that the total rejection they received was unwarranted. Unwarranted, unless the people I was trying to convince were already way ahead of me. I know some of them personally and they are not the type of people to leave any possibility unexplored, no matter how farfetched. They would never simply dismiss an argument (as they did) unless they already knew it to be true, unless the answers to my questions were not for me to know. But, Mike, my nature, my profession, my very life is seeking the truth; I cannot accept any denial of knowledge. Therefore, I bypassed in particular, but not in general, the normal way things are done within this organization.

I will spare you the trivial details of how I accomplished my final end, although almost none of my techniques were honorable. You remember the old saying about the ends never justifying the means? Well, it appears that for our present enterprise that old law has found its exception. I've done quite a bit of amateur philosophizing in the past week and I have come to the conclusion that from the very beginning of this, the most necessary attribute of any of our coconspirators has been a moralistic denial of that statement. We all believe at the foundations of our egos that the ends (as long as we believe them to be righteous) do indeed justify any and all means we deem necessary to acquire them.

You may wonder why I have delved so far into the cauldron of our group's psychology; but after all, isn't it what this is all about. Doesn't someone understand us much better than we understand ourselves? Or is that someone not a single person at all, but some weird gestalt of thousands of human brains and miles of computer circuitry? I don't know the answers as I'm just beginning to grasp the questions. What I do understand is our final goal, so I wish you luck in your mission, and God's guidance in making your decisions concerning the information I now give you.

Enclosed are some documents I procured from the Bloc Systems computer (the same one that found you). Very few men have seen (or should see) these articles, but I think you should be one of them. I pray that my action is correct.

Again, God bless.

Joe Barkman

P.S. This is a very incriminating communication, but I had no other alternative. I trust you will deal with it accordingly.

BLOC SYSTEMS LOG

JOB 3856 FILE RECALL   BEGINNING EXEC – CLASS AAA
JOB 3856 FILE RECALL   RICHARDSON, NORTON R. PH.D.
JOB 3856 END EXECUTION.

COST OF JOB $3.21 – CPU TIME .57 MIN. – 25 LINES PRINTED.

File Summary: Dr. Norton R. Richardson
Born July 9, 1924 Herrington, Kansas. Lived with relatives in Hutchinson, Kansas while attending high school there. Worked way through University of Wisconsin with part time jobs and partial scholarship. Graduated with honors in 1944. Performed postgraduate work at Cornell University 1944-1950. Worked on several projects focusing on bacterial genetics (See unabbreviated file for list of publications), in particular the transformation of non-virulent strains into their virulent analogs.

Married April 23, 1949. Only child born May 5, 1952 (see files – Sally Anne Richardson, Ann Marie Richardson). Post doctorate work done University of California, Berkeley 1952-1954. Research vector change to virology. Was retained at the university as an instructor; obtained tenure and became full professor in 1962.

Research since centers on viral genetics. Bulk of grant money coming from U.S. Dept. of Defense . . . Declared legally dead February 10, 1976. However, BLOC intelligence places him in secret research complex in Southern Libya (see files – Tibesti Highlands Personnel; Selective Avery Genocide in Chad; Air France Flight 342 – victim identification).

BLOC SYSTEMS LOG
JOB 4297 FILE RECALL   BEGINNING EXEC – CLASS AAA
JOB 4297 FILE RECALL   RICHARDSON, SALLY A.
JOB 4297 END EXECUTION.
COST OF JOB $2.29 – CPU TIME .41 MIN. – 22 LINES PRINTED.
File Summary: Sally Anne Richardson

Born May 5, 1952 Ithaca, New York. Moved to Berkeley, California with parents while still in infancy (see files –Dr. Norton R. Richardson, Anne Marie Richardson). Remained there until leaving for San Diego State University in 1970 where she majored in Chemistry. Upon her graduation from college in 1974, she immediately began post graduate work at the University of Illinois in the field of biochemistry . . .

Engaged to be married in December, 1975 (Fiancé married another woman five months after her reported death) . . . while traveling in Europe with her parents . . . Declared legally dead . . . However . . . in Southern Libya . . . (see files . . . .

B radley read Joe's letter over and over again, then as Joe had known he would, fired it up, saving only the computer generated dossiers that could not be connected to him. He put them in a chest pocket and zipped it up just as the Russian came back into the cabin. The captain took a long look at the smoldering ashes on the table and then laughed. *I could get to like this guy,* Bradley told himself, knowing he already did.

"So you try to sink my ship?" He came over to the table. "We have special devices for such things in our Navy."

"Yes, I suppose you do, but I'm not in your Navy, am I?" Bradley looked him in the eyes as he picked up the knife from the table, delaying its return to the sheath just long enough to make the captain uncomfortable.

"It is in these times of great science the mere act of burning documents is sometimes insufficient, the ashes should really be dissolved in acid afterward . . . if one doubts his company." He looked down at the crinkled black ashes on his table. "But, in this case I can only offer this . . ."

Suddenly his big hand slammed down on top of the pile, a small puff of gray mist jumping into the air. Then with his hand still on the ashes, he began to laugh from deep in his diaphragm. Bradley joined him when he lifted his blackened hand to reveal a fine, gray powder on the table that he promptly blew away with one huge birthday candle breath.

Bradley decided that the less he mingled with the crew of the Russian vessel, the less chance there would be of him over staying his welcome, so he requested that his dinner be brought to the captain's quarters. He knew that the meal could very well be his last, and that he would need the nourishment for the activities to come, but he just wasn't hungry. His stomach was in a knot and his mind a torrent of meaningless images. He lay on his back in the darkness, the thoughts coming and going of their own accord. One moment he was with Sharon in his room, the next he was sitting alongside a broken motorcycle in the middle of the Mojave Desert, the next he was trying to sleep in a rice paddy in Vietnam. He couldn't get it together. He wanted the time to pass. He wanted to start to do what he had come so many miles to do. He wanted to occupy his mind in some way. Even if the price paid was death.

The captain came for him himself. He didn't speak. He simply stood by the open door patiently. Bradley checked his equipment one last time, then passed by him into the open corridor. They walked silently.

On the flight deck was a single plane painted a dull shade of gray. The jet engine was revving and the canopies were open. In the forward of the two seats sat the pilot looking monstrous in his helmet and oxygen mask. Bradley was led to the plane and helped into the seat harness and his own headgear and mask. As the canopy closed, the captain saluted and briskly turned away. The engine roared and Bradley was thrust back into the thickly padded seat. Suddenly, they were in the air, flying just above the waves. Forty minutes later, after seeing a lot of desert very close up, the plane shot up in a near vertical climb.

"Good Luck American." WHAM! The canopy overhead was gone and he was rocketing upward and away from the plane in a seventy degree climb. In one infinite second the acceleration ceased and as he began a slow silent tumble the seat belt broke free. He kicked himself away from the seat just as the small pilot chute pulled the navy blue main parachute into the effect of the gale force winds. He had lost sight of the plane, but he knew that the pilot had, as planned, returned to low altitude upon his successful departure. No radar would detect him on his way out. Bradley felt suddenly very alone, almost abandoned. His normally clear head was clouded with thoughts of his new reality; the reality that was floating in the late night sky, over an unforgiving land occupied by unforgiving men; the truism that he was falling slowly downward to a place and time of death, doing so without any other recourse.

The underground laboratory complex had been built roughly in the shape of a cone and consisted of six levels. The first and closest level to the surface contained the security division. All the most advanced electronic equipment used to protect the site was located on Level One. The second level down, Level Two, provided living quarters and mess facilities for the security force that manned that equipment twenty-four hours of each day. Between Level Two and Level Three was a single stairway. Elevators serviced the lower, laboratory levels, but the only means of passage between Levels Two and Three was that one stairwell. It was doubly guarded at both levels.

The stairway down to the laboratory levels was only rarely used, and then only one man could use it at will. This man, a full colonel, was head of the security division. Although the colonel had no "direct" control over the research staff, all passage between Levels Two and Three required his personal approval. All messages leaving the site passed over his desk first. All news from the outside world was censored by him before its distribution to the research staff. Therefore the colonel did exert sizeable control, albeit not literally speaking, directly.

The third level below the surface, Level Three, provided living accommodations for the research staff, an extensive library — 80% of which was stored on microfilm, recreation lounge and dining facilities. Kitchen duties were assigned to less essential members of the research group. The site was resupplied every six months by air, with an extra two months supply always on hand as a buffer against emergencies. The lower three levels, Levels Four, Five and Six, were the reason for the base's existence, they housed the laboratories proper.

Complete biology, biochemistry, bio-inorganic chemistry, organic chemistry, and biophysics facilities were available. The laboratories were complete with all the most modern, and expensive, analytical tools needed to produce viable results. The most liberally staffed sections were the biochemistry and biology laboratories, as the site's research was very directional. Molecular genetics and virology were given top priority.

The questions: Could a specific, genetically similar portion of a given species be attacked biologically, in such a way as to be lethal to that portion, and yet harmless to the remainder? If so, *how?*

Through testing in the laboratory on drosophila, rats, and dogs, and finally by an uncontrolled test in the wild on a randomly chosen species of local birds; the answer to the first question had been shown to be an unqualified, *Yes.* The second question, the *how?* had from necessity, been answered in order to answer the first.

S weat ran into his eyes, but Bradley was far too exhausted to lift his arm up to wipe it away. His throat was parched from the dusty dry air, but he knew if he stopped before reaching the top, he would never make it. He looked up from his boots; there were a few stunted bushes, a few large rocks, and about a hundred meters of ground between him and the top of the hill. He preferred looking down at the ground; watching the ground move by, he felt a little more like he was making progress. He tried to regulate his breathing — inhale, count three — exhale, count three — inhale, count to three. His lungs tried to burst and he gave it up, panting rapidly the rest of the way up the steep slope.

Bradley didn't really care what was on the other side of the ridge; when he reached the rim he simply dropped to his behind and tried to catch his breath. He reached for the wrong canteen and didn't notice it was empty until taking a deep drink of air. He threw it up and away from himself, too tired and dry to even think. It arced high into the air before falling into the valley below. The other canteen was about half empty, he could have finished his remaining water easily, but thinking better of it, he took one deep warm swallow then put the rest away with a sigh. He was wiping his face with a sweaty neckerchief when he noticed that the tiny valley in front of him was vaguely familiar.

"These are the most detailed pictures to date." The red arrow twitched slightly. "This is the entrance as seen two days ago, however, we received photos this morning that show it has since been effectively camouflaged." The arrow jerked to another point, then settled back to twitching. "However, if you will notice the landmarks . . ."

The general curve of the valley, the rock outcropping at the far end, the distribution of vegetation; no mistaking it, Bradley was there. He decided to wait until dark before trying to get any closer. He had been walking most of the night, and he needed to get some sleep, if he possibly could. He chose a likely bush and stuck as much of his upper body as possible into its shadow. He ran out of water just before dusk.

The radar technician sitting watch that morning was uncommonly young for a position of such responsibility, yet his aptitude and intensive training from foreign experts had made him equal or superior to any of the other radar operators who patrolled the rim of the small valley. He was keenly aware of the hundreds of electronic images that represented every rock and bush on the rim. He reported any change in status, any deviation from the norm, however slight. He had on innumerable occasions reported the sightings of small animals and birds. For an instant he thought that this sighting too was the flight of some local bird, but only for an instant. It had appeared suddenly at ground level, arcing to a maximum height of ten to fifteen meters above the rim, then continued its arc into the valley. The arc had been a textbook example of the parabolic curves common to ballistics. The technician motioned his watch leader to come over to his station. A video tape reply was examined and an all systems alert was ordered when the projectile's human source was discovered.

Although the base commander's perpetually black stubbled face appeared granite during his walk from the electronic observation center on security division's first floor, the colonel found the idea of a single man being sent against him and his security team very amusing. He smiled inwardly as he remembered the spy mysteries he had read while learning to speak English.

At the first guard station and door he was passed with facial recognition only. The guard knew him well. The first security door closing behind him, he walked the short distance up the corridor to the second guard station. The colonel was angered by the first guard's breach of security and as he paced off the final few meters to the guard post at the top of the stairs he decided to give the guard on duty there a small test. He returned the guard's crisp salute without slowing his pace and continued on toward the door blocking his way to the stairwell leading down to the laboratory levels.

"One moment, sir," The guard spoke as he stood, "I'm sorry to bother you, but I'll need to see your I.D."

"I don't have time for that right now, Sergeant," the colonel said impatiently as he continued toward the door at the top of the stairs. But with the sure air of a battle hardened veteran, the guard shifted to block his way; an almost imperceptible movement of his hand toward his holster let the colonel know he meant business.

"Sure, Sergeant. I know the rules," he said, slowing to produce his I.D. As he started toward the stairs, the guard shook his head and returned to his post, wondering why the man who had made the rules felt it necessary to expound his knowledge of them. The guard opened the door remotely with his key.

At the foot of the stairwell, and once again at the other end of the corridor leading from it, the colonel was again required to show his identification before his passage forward was permitted. He made a mental note to have the first guard reprimanded for his breach of security. Once through the lower corridor the colonel entered a small room containing yet another guard; security required he remain in this small waiting room until clearance from the Security Control Room on Level One opened this last and most formidable door.

The colonel showed his identification once again and the guard, seated behind a metal desk, recorded the exact time of his passage. The security personnel up in the Security Control Room on Level One had carefully followed their superior's downward passage. They watched, with closed circuit eyes, all movement along that stairway and were quick to give their clearance and remotely open the final door to the research levels.

The heavy metal door slid silently aside and then back closed, leaving the colonel standing with his back to the forward wall of the Level Three dining room. All eyes in the room were on him as he scanned the lunching scientists for the man he had come to see. There sitting at a small table in one of the far corners of the room, slightly removed from the rest of the scientists, was Doctor Norton Richardson with his wife and daughter. The colonel strode smugly over to them and without waiting for an invitation, pulled up a chair to join them.

The colonel spoke first, "Good morning, Doctor Richardson, Mrs. Richardson, Miss Richardson." He gave them each a friendly glance as he called their names, as if reading from some obscure roster. His eyes surveyed hungrily as his glance toward Sally Richardson lasted slightly longer than the ones tossed to her parents.

"Don't wait for us to tell you how glad we are to see you . . . We're not!" Sally Richardson spat the words, causing her mother to wince.

"SALLY!" her father cut in, "What is it you want, Colonel? Our work is proceeding at the expected rate; we simply can't work faster, not and stay within safe limits."

"Work, work, work, you scientists are always thinking about work. This is a social visit, Doctor."

"Thanks, but no thanks," sneered the Doctor's daughter.

"Now, Sally." The colonel knew how much it bothered the girl for him to use her first name. "Is that any way for you to speak to your host?"

"In English, the word you want is warden."

"Now, now, Sally, I came all the way down here to tell you and your wonderful family that you have a visitor, and you treat me thus? I shudder to think how you treat someone who is your enemy when you are like this to your friends." The colonel laughed dryly when she remained silent, her face red with anger.

"What is it you mean by a visitor, Colonel?" the Doctor asked.

"Oh, the man who is waiting patiently up on the rim for it to become dark, of course." Another dry laugh. Richardson tried to phrase his next question in such a way as to yield the most information.

"Does that mean, when you capture him, we will be allowed to speak with him?"

"No, I'm sorry Doctor, but I don't plan on capturing him at all." The colonel called a halt to the conversation by rising and replacing the chair he had brought up to the table. "Good bye, I hope to see you all again very soon, but now I have to welcome our new guest." He began his walk back across the room to the metal door.

"Daddy, we have to do it now. We just can't let them kill whoever it is up there." Sally Richardson almost begged as she looked to see how far the colonel had gone.

"But the door, Sally, what about the Goddamned door. We've been through all this before and nothing has changed."

"It has changed, Daddy, that's why we have to do it now. Whoever that man is up on the rim has probably come to help get us out of here. If we let that bastard kill him we might never get out, but if we act now that man on the rim is going to come down here tonight and open that fucking door." Her mother started at the filthy language. Sally stared at her father and fellow researcher, her arguments exhausted.

"And if he doesn't come down, or if they have already killed him, or if this is just another way for the colonel to torment us?"

"We still won't have lost anything. If worse comes to worse, we can blow the damned door ourselves."

"If he comes down and we don't get to him in time?" Doctor Richardson's last protest sounded feeble as he was almost convinced.

"We will, Daddy. We have to, he came to save *us*." Her father looked to his wife for support. She had remained quiet during the heated argument, but indicated her approval of the plan with one short sentence.

"He's almost to the door, you had better hurry," she said.

Doctor Richardson caught up with the colonel just as he was reaching for the elevator call button.

"Colonel, there is one more thing I must talk to you about." The colonel stopped and turned to face the voice. "I would just have to call you back down, so I think we should take care of it now." Richardson began to lead the colonel back toward the table, and more importantly, closer to the elevator leading down to the laboratories. "The message I tried to send out the other day was imperative to our work. Either you let me send it or tell someone on the outside of the problem."

"What message? I don't recall that you tried to send a message."

"You know. The order for the laboratory supplies you said we didn't need."

"I was told you have everything you need."

"We did, but now we have a new problem. Oh, come see for yourself, it will only take a minute." Leading the colonel into the elevator, Richardson was thankful his women had had the foresight to leave the table the two men had just passed.

Richardson's mind raced during the short trip to the lab. *Down to Level Four by elevator, then on foot the rest of the way to the virology laboratories. Across the lab to the refrigerators, top shelf in the back. Last chance to back out.*

"The agar has all been going bad. If you would just put through my order form for some industrially prepared agar from the United States or Europe, we wouldn't have to worry about it" *Reach in, take the Petri dish out, uncover it nonchalantly.* "Look at this mess." Doctor Richardson thrust his first finger into the agar dish before pushing the dish toward the colonel. "Go ahead, feel it, it's only mold, but it screws up everything" . . . *Do it, DO IT* . . . "Go ahead, feel it."

The colonel cautiously ran his finger over the plate. Richardson began rubbing the agar between his thumb and first finger. "Like this. Feel it like this and you'll know just how bad it is."

"Just give me the order form." The colonel hastily wiped his hands with his handkerchief. "What do I know of such things?"

"Nothing, Colonel. Nothing at all." Richardson moved quickly to a desk, removed an order form, filled it in, and handed it to the colonel to take with him to the upper levels. Richardson's thoughts turned grim, the order form was not the only thing the colonel would bring with him to the security levels.

At sunset, Bradley watched a stubborn sun delay its departure by igniting the night sky. Long after the arson had gone, the horizon was blanketed with a thick layer of glowing red fire. Trapped between the inferno below, and a limitless expanse of icy blackness above, a buffering layer of baby blue struggled for existence. With infinite weight the blackness pressed down, forcing the powerless blue into the flames. Gradually the transient fire thinned and died, the victorious blue filling the void. For a time only blue and black shared the sky. Yet, still the omnipotent blackness pressed on. The same dark weight that had allowed the blue to quench its burning adversary relentlessly drove toward the ground. Then there was only blackness.

Bradley ate a piece of jerky and some high protein bars from his knapsack before hiding it in a bush. The dry food made him curse himself for not saving some water to wash it down. He moved slowly down the incline toward the laboratory entrance, keeping as close to the ground as he could without crawling. The door that was so well camouflaged from air surveillance was easy to find once he grew close, even in the darkness engulfing it. He unzipped the thigh pockets of the jump suit. From one he withdrew a small cardboard carton that held a half pound of plastic explosive. From the other pocket came the detonator. He removed the explosive from the carton and peeled off its protective cellophane. He set the charge and scurried to a safe distance. He assembled the submachine gun from parts taken from various pockets on calves, arms, and chest, slung it by the strap over his head and under his right arm so it was easy to bring to bear, and then unclipped from his belt both of the hand grenades he had brought. Their weight, that had seemed so unbearable during the trek in, felt suddenly too light. Much too light for the unknown that lay coiled to strike behind that door so soon to blow open. It was too late to think of such things. The door would come open and when it did, he must fight or die. He armed the grenades by removing their safety wires and held one in each trembling hand, fingers gripping and re-gripping their smooth round surfaces, searching for the perfect hold. They never found it.

The silent blackness was shattered by a blinding roar as the metal door yielded to the explosion, tore off the door frame and flew inward. A second later he stood at the torn and twisted metal of the entrance and threw in the two spheres of death. Diving to one side, his impact with the dirt was accompanied by an ear ringing concussion. The simultaneous detonation of the two bombs shook the ground for a long instant. By the time it had stopped he again stood in the doorway that led into the rock fortress, weapon poised to fire.

Through a haze of dust and smoke, the single incandescent light fixture that remained intact shed a feeble gray light. One by one, other sources of yellow orange light flickered to life as electronic control panels sparked into small, smoky flames. As the ringing in his ears retreated he began to hear the sparking of the damaged panels. A muffled alarm sounded somewhere below, warning of his coming. There were ten or twelve bodies in the room. Some were still draped over their panels, but most lay scattered about the floor.

He picked his way through the room, avoiding debris and bodies, moving toward the origin of the alarm. The alarm would sound – *Arruga* – pause, then sound again. As he moved across the room it grew louder. Not gradually, but with an audible increase in intensity with each sounding. As if it knew he was coming closer and cried louder, as if to impart more urgency to its call with every step he took.

114

It seemed to cry out a tortured question, "Who are you? Who are you?" Then the light went out.

He unclipped the flashlight from his belt. Holding it, but not turning it on, he realized what a good target he would make in a dark room holding a light. Then he became aware that the sparking had stopped at the same time the light had gone out. The light hadn't just been turned off, the power had been cut. *If they have power doors,* he thought, I *won't be able to get through.* He looked back toward where the alarm was sounding. A vertical rectangle of light hung in the darkness. He turned on the flashlight and began to move toward what he realized was a half-open door. When he was almost there, it began to rain. The small fires sizzled out as he reached the doorway. He surmised that the power cut and sprinklers were part of some automated fire sequence. The automatic door would have slid completely closed as part of that sequence, had not a body been wedged in the opening.

He looked through the doorway into the light and saw a short, brightly lit hallway leading to an elevator. Midway down the hall was a desk. On either side of the desk floor-to-ceiling, heavy-gage wire-mesh fences blocked his passage. Two more disturbing things were in the hallway. At the desk and at the elevator end of the hall were two more guards to match the first one he had found stuck in the doorway. They also appeared dead. He stepped cautiously through the door, knowing his grenades could not have penetrated this far, keeping his machine gun aimed in their direction.

When he got near the fence, he fired into the guard slumped at the desk. Neither body moved so he assumed them to be genuinely dead. He shot the first gate open with a short burst, opened the second gate with the desk guard's keys and then checked the guard at the elevator. He was dead, but Bradley could see no obvious reason for his death. No blood. No wounds.

Bradley began to worry; he wasn't prepared for the silent, invisible death he had found. He couldn't avoid the conclusion that these people had made some fatal error. They hadn't taken the proper precautions; they had played with biological weapons and had killed themselves with them. The part that sent the chill up Bradley's spine was the knowledge that they had killed him too.

The elevator controls were on the desk — four buttons: Up, Down, Open and Close. He could tell from the simple up and down arrows that it only serviced this and one other floor; most probably the next one down. The problem was this: He could call the elevator up, or send it down as he pleased, but once it was up at this level, another button on the desk had to be pushed to open the doors. The doors would only open if the door button was pushed after the elevator had arrived. That he could do. What he could not do was get from the desk to the open elevator before the doors reclosed. He propped the guard at the elevator up in a sitting position with his back against the closed doors. The next time he opened the doors, the guard fell across the tracks. When the doors closed, his body prevented a complete seal and the doors were blocked open.

Bradley was inside the elevator, tugging at the body, when something compelled him to stop and think. He stood erect and examined the inside of the elevator for the first time. No controls. If he let the doors close without someone to order the elevator to descend, he would be locked in that box at the same level for the rest of his short life.

He was dying; he knew that whatever it was that had killed the guards was at that moment killing him. But Bradley was Irish, and the Irish are a very stubborn people. He had come to blow up this complex so it could never be used again and to kill anyone who knew its secret of genocide. Well, they themselves had saved him the trouble of killing them, but he still had to blow the place up and do it in such a way that all the infected bodies, including his own, would be incinerated. He stepped back out of the elevator and walked slowly to the desk.

I may be able to rig something here to send it down, he thought, *but damn it, if they have the same system down there, I'll still be locked in.* Being at the lower level wouldn't help him unless he could get out of the elevator.

"Well, Mickey." He sighed out loud. "You really don't have much of a goddamned choice now do ya?" He looked through the desk drawers until he found a ruler. He used some masking tape to shape one end of the ruler into a large pad. Then he sat the guy at the desk up in his chair, placed the padded end of the ruler on the arrow that pointed down, and stuck the other end in the guard's mouth.

Once in the elevator, he pulled the body from the doors and pushed it into the hallway. If he did spend the rest of his time in that cube, he didn't really want to do it with a dead body. The doors closed down on his boot, leaving just a crack of an opening. He aimed for the middle of the desk guard's back and as he fired he pulled his foot from the doors. He never saw the guard fall forward as the doors had already closed, but when he felt himself become slightly weightless he knew he had.

He didn't draw breath during the minute or so it took the elevator to reach the lower level. As it slowed to a stop, he could feel his heart pounding in his throat. The elevator came to a complete stop and nothing happened. The few moments between the elevator's halt and the doors sliding open had seemed an eternity, but open they finally did.

The elevator at this level was operated by a call button on the wall outside the doors. One push would bring the elevator down. When it got to this level, the doors opened and stayed open for a moment. After this moment, the doors reclosed and the elevator rose to the upper level. Once it arrived at the upper level, the doors were manually opened by the guard at the desk in the hallway. That is, if the closed circuit camera in the elevator proved to the guard's satisfaction that the passenger was authorized to be at the top level. However, the guard at that desk would never again operate those controls.

This level was much larger than the one above. It had barracks to accommodate about fifty men. There were many bodies here, but Bradley didn't stop to count them. There was a combination kitchen and dining room that was small enough to make him believe the men ate in groups of ten or fifteen. There was a fairly large recreation room that looked like it was capable of passing a lot of boring hours for a lot of lonely men.

The armory was the next room he entered. The top of the Dutch door was open so he climbed over, stepping over the clerk to get inside. It was large and well stocked. As he looked at the various weapons and thought about the many bodies strewn about on this level and the one above, he realized that if the security force of this base had not already been dead upon his arrival, he could have never gotten past the first door. Maybe not even that far. He began to wonder if the people he worked for had expected it would be like this. Then it all made sense.

Joe Barkman had told him during their discussion on the plane. He had told him in such a way that he wouldn't ever understand unless he did get this far. He had told Bradley of his friend being kidnapped and brought here to work against his will. He had told him in a way that it wouldn't take on its real meaning until right now. The entire plan had from the start depended on Bradley receiving help from the scientist they believed to be imprisoned somewhere below. If the scientist wasn't here, or if he couldn't find a way to help, well then Bradley would get killed so quick that there would be very little chance of him screwing things up. The status would be much as it was before his arrival and they would just try something else.

"Those people are goddamned phenomenal." He spoke aloud as he came to a rack of Czech made AK-47 rifles. He chose one and sought ammunition. He left his lighter, less powerful weapon in exchange. He found some boxes of Russian grenades and clipped four to his belt. He didn't expect to find anyone alive and looking for a fight, but there would probably be more locked doors or gates.

He left the armory and walked down another hallway. There were conventional doors on either side that led into apartment like rooms. Three were locked, but the locks were designed for privacy not defense and a kick opened the doors easily. These were unoccupied, the men who lived in them had not been home when whatever happened, had happened. Two more were open and had dead junior officers in them. The last was much larger than the others and a colonel was sprawled out next to a large oak desk. Bradley stood looking down at what he was sure was the base commander. It wasn't a very glorious way for a soldier to die.

At the end of the corridor was a sliding metal door and a guard at a small desk. On the desk there was an electronic lock with a key in it; he turned it from stop to stop but the door didn't open. He supposed it was some safety feature due to the destruction of the first level. He backtracked the corridor to one of the open doorways and from it threw one of the grenades at the door at the end of the hall. It blew the door away easily and as he passed through the wreckage, he knew that this level's destruction, and possibly the two contiguous, could be arranged by blowing the armory. He walked down another, shorter corridor. At the far end were desk and door identical to the first. He didn't bother looking for the key before blowing it.

Behind the door was a stairwell leading downward. The door at the foot of the stairwell opened with a burst of machine gunfire. After passing through another bland corridor that duplicated the one upstairs, he blew the door at the other end with another grenade. A small waiting room was on the other side. The room was nearly empty: another metal desk, a wheeled desk chair and another dead man. The chair was upright, but it was against the far wall. The dead man lay outstretched on the floor a short distance from the desk. Some sort of ledger book was at his side.

The door opposite Bradley was conspicuous in its uniqueness from the others with which he had so easily dealt. It was much larger and seemed to have been forged from a single piece of metal. The longer he looked at that door, the more convinced he was that the laboratory proper was just on the other side. However he wasn't at all sure that one grenade would grant him passage. It became apparent, when he could find no device, mechanical or electronic, within the anteroom, that the door was remotely controlled from parts unknown.

He knew that the door's control would not be from the other side of the massive barricade and that the door blocked outgoing as well as incoming traffic with identical efficiency. It would be up to him to remove it. He had decided to try the final grenade first, then return to the armory for more explosives if necessary, when curiosity got the better of him.

He picked up the ledger book to see what the dead man had been recording when he died. It appeared to be a running record of who passed through the door and when. Bradley could only read the numbers, but that was enough; the last passage through the door had been just under eight hours earlier. Someone had entered, stayed about an hour, and within eight hours of coming came back out everyone on this side of the door was dead. He checked the time since first coming through the ground level door — one hour fifty-seven minutes. That led to the inescapable conclusion that he had a maximum of about six hours left. Most probably a lot less. He tried to swallow, but he couldn't.

He took cover at the doorway leading back upstairs and threw the grenade. After the explosion he tried to see if there had been any effect. His eyes would not focus and at first he thought it was a result of the blast, but it lasted too long. He was definitely seeing double and couldn't straighten himself out. He closed his eyes and gave them a rough rub with the backs of clenched fists. When he tried to reopen them he got another shock; his eyelids seemed to be made of lead. Slowly, using all his will power, he gradually managed to raise them to a drooping half-open position, only to find he was still seeing double. And his throat had become very uncomfortable from not being able to swallow.

He realized he had grossly overestimated the time it was going to take for him to die. He turned to start back to the armory, thinking he could at least blow it and thereby seal access to the lower levels, but as he moved, his legs began to go rubbery. He took one unstable step and fell. His entire body felt like Jell-O. He tried to get up, but to no avail. All his voluntary muscle control was yielding to some unknown paralysis. Then he remembered something that would have made him scream in terror had he still possessed the ability to scream. Breathing is a reflex controlled by voluntary muscles. The terror that was bottled inside him grew on itself and multiplied until there was nothing left of his rational mind. No thoughts, no memories, no time; only the timeless, mindless, synergism of combined terror and panic. Finally, he ceased to breathe and was soon engulfed by blackness.

L ooking down, the sand was damp from the predawn mist. Up, the sun was beginning to boil off that same mist as it sat impatiently on the rolling horizon. The sand crunched softly under the two soldiers' boots as they climbed the gentle slope of the dune. Upon reaching the sandy plateau, the two men turned to survey the transient valley these gigantic, yet temporary, mountains had formed. As the sun rose higher, the metallic shadows took on more discernible shapes. There was little movement now, for breakfast had been eaten and the camp broken while the sun was still hours away from the rim of this part of the world. Camouflage netting no longer concealed the massive tan shapes as the sun shone more vertically into the valley.

This day had been imminent for months and these men had been here waiting for it over a week. General Riley looked to his aide as if he would speak, but the deathly silence was torn by the sound of a single American Jeep leaping into life. The Jeep roared up the dune. Upon its arrival, the two men climbed in and again the General began to speak.

"Today we will find out if . . ." The rest of his speech was smothered by the deafening thunder an armored division creates as it simultaneously fires up on that last tick of every synchronized watch.

Miraculously, as the Jeep raced down to the warming machines of war, the deep throated rumble was drowned in the high pitched scream of jet engines. Waves of Russian carrier-based fighter bombers flew over, just a few hundred feet above the tanks, their wing tips dipping this way and that in playful salute. A few arms waved back from the ground, but most were too nervous for such games.

Bradley was awake, but he couldn't move, speak or open his eyes. He didn't even possess the ability to breathe on his own. His heart was pounding, but with each assisted breath it grew less violent. He realized, groggily, that someone was administering artificial respiration, mouth to mouth. He could hear a distant voice, but only in jagged pieces did meaning come through to him.

". . . coming around now . . . another injection . . . no inhibitor this time . . ." He felt a pin prick in his right arm. One eyelid was opened, but he perceived only light, and then the lid was closed. He felt a desire to cough, but only a weak exhalation with accompanying choke would come. More voices. "Turn him over and let him clear his lungs." He was rolled onto his stomach and a different type of respiration resumed. The next time he coughed it was a deep, powerful cough; wet with accumulated mucus. He began to breathe by himself.

"He'll be all right now," a female voice said. He lay on his belly until he had the strength to roll over by himself. He opened his eyes wondering if he had been captured or saved. A fleeting hope that maybe the whole thing had been a product of delirium was extinguished when his sight finally focused on the same corridor he had last seen before blacking out.

"So you have come back to us." He turned his head toward the unexpected voice, the woman's voice, to see a slight girl in her mid-twenties sitting Indian fashion next to him.

He tried to speak, but only got out one word, "Richardson?" It was enough to transmit meaning. Her blue eyes lit up and she glanced around herself, as though she wanted to share the moment with someone else, someone who evidently was not around.

"Yes. We are the Richardsons, the people you have come to save." He tried to speak, but nothing intelligible came forth.

"Now you just rest until you get your strength back. You were poisoned by a bacteriological toxin, but you're all right now. The bacteria are gone and the toxin neutralized."

Bradley's mind went back to college and a page in a microbiology textbook came vividly back to him. A graph relating cell population and the amount of toxin they produced had been on that page. He realized that these people had saved his life, but it didn't seem to matter. He only wanted to know if the organism was the same one he had been sent ten thousand miles to destroy.

"How? I have the background to understand the details." He added the last as an afterthought, knowing that a scientist avoids talking science to anyone who needs to be spoon fed ideas.

"On our own time here, we developed a new bacterium from several species of 'Bugs' made available to us for the work we were being forced to do. We called it 'No Alternative' because we knew we would only use it as a last recourse. It was our only weapon in the event of the completion of their big project. We only delayed using it because we didn't know what lay beyond the door, or even where we are. So we waited for someone to come and try to get us out. Someone like you, who could come in from the other end and open that damn door."

"Did I . . . ?"

"No, we heard an explosion, but the door didn't open. When nothing happened after that, we figured you had died from the bug we had released. We had been preparing to blow the door anyway, so we went ahead. We used a big vat of concentrated perchloric acid, and granulated plastic. Crude, but as you can see, effective." He couldn't help but smile when he saw the mess their makeshift bomb had made out of the door and wall. There must have been a better way.

"Not bad. You must have gotten to me pretty fast. From what I saw upstairs, there isn't much time between first symptoms and death."

"That was the hard part. The organism had to spread rapidly enough that the entire base was infected before the first fatality, and the first and last deaths could only be a few minutes apart. That's why we chose the most mobile carrier possible, the base commander. He probably had the entire base infected ten minutes after we gave it to him. It is airborne and infiltrates the body through the nasopharyngeal membranes."

"What about you?" He felt spongy and weak; his lungs seemed to have only part of their normal volume.

"Oh, we immunized ourselves against 'No Alternative' weeks ago. You were the problem we hadn't foreseen."

"So how come I'm alive?" He coughed again and a huge amount of phlegm tried to choke him.

"Well, since we couldn't inoculate you up front, we knew we would have to treat you for both the infection and the toxin already in your system. The infection was nothing, but the toxin already in circulation was more complicated. We shot you full of pooled antibody serum and injected an acetylcholine esterase inhibitor in small amounts until we started to get some voluntary muscle response from you."

"From what I know about neurotoxins and nerve synapse biochemistry, what you're telling me sounds like a shot in the dark." He was trying not to act too impressed, but not doing a very good job.

"Since we knew the exact point of action of the toxin, inhibition of acetyl choline production, we had a small, but definite chance for success."

"It looks like it worked." He sat up slowly and with great effort. "A little anyway."

"Oh, you'll be all right in a little while if you just relax. I'm going to get my parents, they went back to get some of our notes and things before we go." She stood up from where she had been kneeling and Bradley realized that she was a very beautiful woman.

Not the scientist type at all. She had very long, very straight blond hair, parted it in the middle with airy bangs that flowed to each side of her small face. Her skin was silky smooth and tinted sand dune beige with an occasional small, rust colored mole. Immense sapphire eyes succeeded in distracting attention from her subtly imperfect features. Her hair fell thickly in a vertical plane to her tiny hips; there it was clipped into a blunt square edge. Her small build seemed somewhat sexually unimpressive, yet with all the golden hair waving and corundum eyes flashing, the unsubstantial body and slightly mismatched features faded mistily from Bradley's mind. She smiled one of those, "I know what you're thinking, but from you I don't mind," smiles a guy gets sometimes if he's lucky, and started to walk away.

"We can't go yet. This complex must be destroyed." She stopped instantly. Bradley forced himself to a wobbly standing position.

"What?! Are you crazy? This place is *not* a healthy place. Even if no more soldiers are to be expected, there are dead bodies everywhere."

"We're just going to have to take our chances. Come here and give me a hand." He leaned on her as they walked through the jagged hole in the wall and into a large dining room. It was littered with dead people. She found some water and Bradley took two of the methedrine pills he had brought with him. Within minutes, his mind and body felt new and ready for work.

"Hey, your name is Sally isn't it? My name is Mike. Do you have an American cigarette?"

"No, but Daddy does. Come on, I'll take you to him."

Bradley ground out the smoldering filter he held regretfully, without trying to take another drag. Sally Richardson stood close to him as she leaned over the table to refill the coffee cups of her parents and their new guest.

"Thank you, Sally." Something in Richardson's voice, or eyes, conveyed a silent message to his women. They both left on the pretense of fixing some sandwiches. "Now what is this Sally tells me of not being able to leave here immediately, Mr. Bradley?"

"The most important facet of my mission here is to insure that this facility is not restaffed and its research goal achieved. I must stay long enough to figure out some way to destroy this place." Richardson's face was blank for a moment, then turned suddenly grim.

"I will show you our labs after we eat." His face became even more sour as he reached for his coffee cup and raised it to his lips. He paused to speak just prior to taking a drink. "We have a very distasteful cleanup job to do before we can use any of them."

They removed the bodies from the laboratory sections to a large refrigerated storage locker without the help of Mrs. Richardson. She had retired to her room when she saw what they were doing. As they worked, Richardson and Sally explained to Bradley some of the points that were still vague to him.

They had indeed been kidnapped and forced to work on the genocide project, but had been dragging their feet as much as they could without being overt. The test run on the birds in Chad had been Richardson's brain child. Richardson had known that the test was unnecessary, but had convinced his co-workers that it would be safer to be sure before trying the virus on its eventual human victims. He had meant it only to expend time, but it had instead sent out a warning beacon. The bird die-off had alerted the Bloc to the fact that the researchers inside the Libyan laboratory were very close to finishing their work. The final bug had been ready for a week before Bradley's arrival, but Richardson had been able to conceal this from some of the more willing researchers in a way he didn't fully divulge.

The bug was a highly infectious virus that spread rapidly throughout a population, a virus that thrived and reproduced in all members of the species, but only proved lethal to the genetically unique portion of the species that possessed the targeted genotype. Through genetic engineering, they had developed a virus that could infect every dog in the world, but be lethal only to the Dalmatian; or every cat, and kill only the Siamese; or every human being, and only destroy those with Oriental traits, African traits, European traits. The choice belonged to those who had the knowledge and technology to manufacture the virus.

The group that had built the laboratory in Libya had chosen all the people of the world with Jewish ancestry as their target victims. The process required only that there was some gene identifying the victim race in an adjacent location on the DNA strand to a gene that coded for the production of a protein necessary for survival of the organism. Since the genetics of Tay Sachs syndrome, a disease predominately of those with Jewish ancestry, had been extensively studied for many years in the attempt to find a cure; the Libyan researchers were given a large head start in their preliminary search for the two genes required by the viral killer.

General Silas Riley's elite fourth armored division had attacked at the first glow of light high in the eastern sky. They had been specifically selected and assigned to their objective because of its crucial importance to the Bloc plan. The installation needed to be completely neutralized within the first hour of the synchronized attacks occurring all along the thin border strips controlled by the UNMEDF. The need for almost instantaneous success was paramount, for if the Israeli intelligence services misinterpreted the lighting strike at their nuclear weapons center, a nuclear first strike at the Arab countries was a terrifying probability. That is why the Fourth Armored Division – flying UNMEDF flags of peace – had drawn continually closer and more accessible to its unsuspecting prey during the days leading up to the coordinated attacks.

Within 50 minutes, the surprise armored strike had neutralized all the center's conventional defensive weapon systems and had penetrated the underground complex where the true prize stood readying.

The Israelis have never been called cowards and on this day they lived up to their tradition in memorable fashion. Yet with specially trained shock troops armed with flamethrowers and devastating short-range, high-kill scatter guns, the Fourth pushed relentlessly on through the tunnels, leaving them charred and broken in their wake.

Sixty-three minutes after the first shots were fired, the Israeli nuclear weapons center had been secured by the successful, yet somehow overly vicious "Fourth." When Riley was sure of victory he sent out his message: "This is Riley — we have secured the target." Out in the fleet crusing on the Mediterranean a Spanish general on the UNMEDF flagship was pleased.

General Alvarez knew that this would be only the first report coming in from his field commanders during the next few hours, and some would probably not be as pleasing, yet an important hurdle had been crossed. Israel no longer had a nuclear capability.

What General Alvarez did not know was that instead of a quick dismantling of the nuclear hardware, the technicians of the somewhat greedy General Riley were reprogramming the delivery systems with new targets and placing the weapons on full alert.

Sally Richardson and Bradley toured the extensive laboratory complex that Arab oil money had financed and aging, but unrepentant, Nazi scientists had organized. It was impressive for a private project. Not only were biological problems being studied, but other more physical problems in explosives, fuels, lasers, radio, radar and metallurgy were also being investigated to a lesser emphasis. For Bradley's purpose, this was the important section of the lab — the section that had the potential to yield the necessary power to make the laboratory a memory.

The air in the organic chemistry lab reeked with the typical head-lightening stench of the more volatile compounds common to that branch of chemistry. Badly stained counter tops and acid blacked cabinets testified to frequent use. A large round bottom flask of some sticky black tar hung from a ring stand, an ugly reminder of what had happened to the researcher running the recently failed reaction.

Bradley searched the laboratory until he found the chemical storeroom; a large padlocked hasp had been torn from the door. The lock hung heavily from the mangled metal.

"Dad pried that off. We took the reagents we needed to blow the main entrance door."

"I hope there is something a little more efficient here. I want this whole place irreparable." Bradley took a cursory inventory of what was available. "Not much to work with, really. Just have to synthesize something and use the armory too." Bradley turned to Sally Richardson. "Too bad they didn't put in a nuclear power plant. That would have made it relatively simple."

"I'm sure the energy for this place comes from fossil fuels, Mike. The way the colonel spoke about unlimited energy, I wouldn't be surprised if the complex is sitting over a natural gas reservoir." Bradley's mind raced to a vision of filling the immense complex with just the right mixture of gas and oxygen to obtain the hottest thermodynamic results.

"Well, let's keep looking; we might see something else."

"You know there is a particle accelerator somewhere in the physical wing. The operators sent up a stink because all they were allowed to do was synthesize isotopes for the use of the inorganic group. They wanted their own project."

"Sometimes that does become a problem . . . even back home." Bradley fought off the thoughts of a time and place in a seemingly distant past. "Let's go to the inorganic lab and see what they were up to."

The inorganic laboratories were spacious. It appeared that almost as many resources had been assigned to this project as had been given to the awesome genetics group. Bradley was intrigued. "I wonder what they were trying to do. We need to find their notes."

The inorganic group had been headed by an ancient, German-speaking scientist who had worked diligently for the cause of the Third Reich until its defeat. He had continued his work for that cause after being moved to Argentina and provided with almost unlimited funds. His notes, of course, were in impeccable order in grammatically correct German. Bradley was again surprised by how much the Bloc knew about him when he began reading the German's notes with almost total fluency.

The goal of the project was incredible: to synthesize an inorganic complex of an unstable isotope with a three dimensional arrangement of liqands that would compel an alpha particle, ejected down a molecular corridor, to a specific internal target. That target was to be multiple tritium nuclei forced into close spatial relationship by molecular structural stress in a pseudo enzymatic manner, thereby overcoming Vanderwall's repulsion of the proton isotopes. The fusion of the target proton isotopes into helium and concurrent energy production was the goal.

Bradley was stunned. He reread the material for long hours while Sally Richardson looked on quietly. Finally she brought him out of his deep concentration with a cup of strong coffee.

"Drink this Michael. If you keep going over the same material like that, you'll only blind yourself with bias."

"No, I think I understand it." He took the coffee and drank deeply. His face contorted as the scalding liquid burned his tongue. "They were very close to what they were seeking. If they had had a decent inorganic chemist, they probably would have beaten the biology group to results."

"What was it, Michael? You look white as chalk."

"This guy," he slapped the dead German's bound notebook with the back of his left hand as he put down the coffee cup he held with his right, "figured out a way to chemically induce nuclear fusion at ridiculously low temperatures . . . and at the level of a single molecule."

"I don't think I understand."

"Well, normally, it takes high heat energy of an environment or kinetic energy of a projectile to overcome the natural repulsion of nuclei before they'll fuse. He got around that by physically pressing them together within the structure of a complex molecule. The maniac was brilliant!"

She still didn't understand the process, but she recognized the term fusion.

"I'm glad we killed him. I'm glad we killed him before it was perfected."

"Yeah, he couldn't compress it enough with the liqands he was trying to use, but he had it finished. All I have to do is substitute a couple of organic liqands . . . all of the radioactive stuff is right."

Sally pushed herself away from the counter where Bradley sat with revulsion.

"You mean to say you're going to complete this mad man's work? You're as deranged as he was!"

"Listen." Bradley turned and grasped her shoulders with both hands. "It's the only way. I couldn't have blown this place with anything else we've found. I need to know that this place will never be dug up and its secrets rediscovered." He looked into her sapphire eyes; his own brown eyes pleading. "And I need your help."

Bradley had been trained by inorganic chemists who still did things by feel. He remembered some of the things they had said. "Once the reaction is started, don't leave it for a second . . . don't take your eyes off of it. If it looks like the reaction is going too fast, cool it off with a Dewar filled with liquid nitrogen." *Fast? How fast is fast?* Or, "You let the stuff cook up until the color changes from normal red to 'good and red.'" *Red? How red is "good and red?"* Or, "Keep feeling the Schlenk tube, if it gets too hot, it's ruined." *Hot? How hot is hot?* At first, Bradley had wanted color wave lengths and temperatures in degrees centigrade, but gradually he realized that these men were skilled craftsmen who depended much on their intuition after first taking full advantage of all the numbers and formula of modern chemistry. Through the close, one-on-one, master-apprentice relationship, Bradley had learned how hot "too hot" was.

The German had left nothing to intuition, exact reaction times and temperatures were there, along with detailed descriptions of failures as well as successful synthesis. A good cook with no knowledge of chemistry could duplicate his recipes, but still not have the creativity required for success.

The yield of their tiny first run was calculated at 92%. Bradley found the largest inert atmosphere glassware on the floor and used all the available starting material in one big sloppy, unwieldy reaction. The yield was 97.4% and they were the proud possessors of five kilos of sparkling kelly green crystals. Crystals, the German had written, that would degrade to not so shiny baby blue powder if it wasn't kept completely dry; baby blue powder that had absolutely no pseudo catalytic activity.

They stored the product in five large desiccators where they could keep it dry and oxygen free by pulling a vacuum on the headspace. Five Pyrex glass jars with ground glass lids for a sure seal and stopcocks to attach the vacuum lines. Pump out the air, replace it with an inert atmosphere and then close the stopcock valves; simple. As they let the product pump down, they sat on a quickly cleared lab counter and leaned back against the wall. Both of them had hot cups of coffee and Bradley smoked. Although Sally Richardson had grown tolerant of Bradley's smoking, she still found the intake of nicotine distasteful.

Bradley had been gazing, dreamily, through the fog of exhaustion at the five half-full desiccators confining the kelly green, crystalline solid. Sally spoke, but Bradley didn't register her meaning, although he heard her quite clearly.

"Pardon me, I wasn't all here."

She laughed with happy blue eyes and full, naturally pink lips. "That's what I asked, where are you?" For the first time in over a week Bradley forgot reality and broke out in loud, almost too loud and uninhibited, laughter. They spilled their coffee and cried with laughter. They fell off the lab bench and bent with the pain of laughter and, finally, after a series of short strained bursts of laughter, became silent and thoughtful.

"Well?" Her voice held a slightly sexual edge.

"I was thinking about what would have happened if there had been a secondary reaction, you know the catalytic reaction, while we were still heating the stuff up. I was wondering if when it caused the fusion reaction, the force would have been enough to take out the entire complex."

"Is that why we made it all at once?" This time there was no flirtation in her voice, only the dry sound of not so well hidden fear.

"That's one of the reasons. The other is that I wouldn't want to run that reaction too many times as tired as we are; that would be asking for an accident. A ruptured Schlenk tube, a faulty stopcock, something we did in the wrong sequence or forgot to do at all — any one of a hundred things could have gone wrong and the risk would have been multiplied by the number of times we had to go through it."

The conversation became morbid and contrasted against the exaggerated humor only minutes passed. He knew the laughter had been more of a hysterical release of pressures accumulated than anything else, yet he longed for a return to that release. He wanted to bury a growing uneasiness with upcoming distasteful events under even the thinnest veil of forced jocularity. He needed much more time with the pressure release valve opened.

"Now that we're finished with that, I can get down to chasing you around the lab a few times. After all, you are the best looking lab assistant in the place." Bradley had been trying to guide her into the age old game of slightly sexual verbal parrying. But Sally Richardson called a halt to the game before it had a chance to develop with wide eyes that emanated a satiny intermingling of womanly dominance and schoolgirl surrender. Her hand found Bradley's and grasped it with the near ambiguity of tenderness and strength.

"If it's the chase you're interested in, Mike, I'm afraid I can't help you." Her eyes held his eyes, her hand held his hand, and her desire was his desire. Yet something dark and ugly was in the room with them, something other than normal sexual considerations or trepidations, it was screaming at Bradley to break her hold, to avoid becoming involved with her. It ebbed and flowed with his attempts at knowing its substance; the closer he looked, the less substantial it became until its evanescence winked into the misty world of memory.

"I have a little wine in my room . . . it will help us relax. Won't you join me?" He knew that the offer was for so much more than a quiet glass of wine with which to unwind. But the familiar elation of expectancy was joined by some darker component of doubt.

"This may not be the right time for anything like that, you know." He was putting up the last fragile defenses he had available and he really didn't know why. Bradley wanted her touch, longed to hold and be held, ached to find a few moments of oblivion making love to her. Yet, something was forcing him to drag his feet.

"There may never be a better time," she said quietly. During all this, she had not released her hold of his eyes or hands, as if to do so would set him adrift from her. Bradley suddenly realized she needed him even more than he so desperately needed her. The last psychological fences fell and the darkness seemed infinitely far away.

"The desiccators need a couple of hours more vacuum, then we can pump in some dry argon to equalize the pressure without letting in any oxygen or water. I could use a little wine and relaxation before we set them up."

136

Sally's room was atypically barren for a sensitive, intelligent woman. The lack of personal knickknacks gave the room a cold, institutional air in spite of the thick carpet and costly furnishings. A thick drape separated the room into a small living room with a velour couch and arm chair set, arranged geometrically around a massive coffee table, and an even smaller bedroom with a door into a tiny bathroom. A bottle of Pouilly Fuisse and two heavy, rough hewn wine glasses stood on the table. Sally's voice intercepted Bradley's thought.

"A girl never knows when she'll have company, does she? I'm afraid it won't be very cold, but as you can see, I don't have a refrigerator." She sat on one end of the couch as she picked up the corkscrew and began the operation of opening the bottle. "I found it in the colonel's office yesterday — he must have more somewhere, but this was the only bottle I could find." The cork popped out and she deftly spun it off the tool.

"You do that like an old hand. Do you do this often?" Bradley felt that the joke might fall sickly, but Sally took it up with happy energy. "Just count the notches in my corkscrew, why don't you." She poured, then put down the bottle before proposing a toast. "Moment to moment." Bradley repeated the phrase and they drank long and deep.

Then they were in each other's arms exploring their mysterious first kiss. They still had their wine glasses clumsily held out behind and away from each other, but neither of them could bare even the shortest pause. Their tongues danced together the elaborate courtship dance of unthinking, uninhibited, unrestrained passion. Long, breathless, excited moments passed before they separated slightly. Sally's tongue whipped softly over his lips, then disappeared into a kiss of each of his lips individually and repeatedly. He kissed her eyelids and her ears, her velvet neck and her silky hair, now shining loosely about her small shoulders; and soon, too soon, their first embrace faded into gazing eyes and small obligatory sips of amazingly unspilled wine.

"We'll be more comfortable in the back," she said quietly, standing with the neck of the bottle and her glass in one hand, while she pulled gently on Bradley's arm with the other. They walked the half dozen steps to the bed, placed their glasses on the bed stand and undressed quickly. They lay down without the burden of clothing or inhibition. They again embraced and kissed, fondled and caressed. Slowly the initial desperation of ardor became the final desperation for success. Sally was beautiful and firm, she was loving and understanding, she was knowledgeable and adept, and Bradley was hopelessly impotent.

The bombardment was increasing. Major Mereeve was in a foxhole with his radio man trying to contact the fleet. At first light three days ago, the Soviet paratroopers had been dropped directly on top of the Syrian missile complex. This had been an error of almost three kilometers and it had cost them many casualties as they had been decimated by anti-aircraft weapons while they were still drifting helplessly downward. Their beloved commander, Colonel Chubikoff, never touched the ground alive. During the first two hours the Russians had fought bravely enough to accomplish their goal — the capture of the tiny Syrian missile base.

The destruction of the biological warheads was to be accomplished by a small nuclear warhead being detonated in the warhead storage locker a quarter of a kilometer underground. But the nuclear destruct mechanism could not be brought in by helicopter until the area was secure; and for two bloody days, the drop zone had been anything but secure. By some freak accident of fate, two Syrian armored divisions being drawn out of Lebanon had been within twenty kilometers of the missile complex when the Soviet paratroopers had so amazingly arrived. The first two hours at the complex had gone as well as could have been expected, considering the poor placement of the drop. But then the Syrian armor had arrived and began the shelling. Only the frequent sorties of Soviet fighter bombers prevented the paratroopers from being immediately overrun. The Syrians had learned a lot about air defense, however, from their continual run-ins with the Israelis. The Soviet air attacks were proving very costly to the small UNMEDF air force.

Major Mereeve had inherited command of the strike force when Colonel Chubikoff had been killed in the jump. He had lost contact with the fleet shortly after the last armored attack and he was desperate to regain his communications. He needed that warhead, and he needed it now. His troops were almost out of anti-tank weapons as they had already repulsed two Syrian armored attacks they had not expected to encounter. They had not been equipped with many heavy weapons before the drop, and Major Mereeve seriously doubted if they could repel another hard pressed attack by infantry and armor. The biological warheads had to be destroyed, incinerated in a thermonuclear explosion, before they could be recaptured by the Syrians. And recaptured they would be if he couldn't regain contact with the fleet. They needed to get that destruct mechanism through to him.

Soviet casualties were already at 40% and growing so fast Major Mereeve couldn't maintain a viable chain of command. Mereeve realized that if he didn't destroy the bio-weapons soon, there wouldn't be enough of the strike force left to accomplish it. At that moment the shelling stopped and he heard a call from a Russian out on the periphery of their shrinking perimeter.

"Here they come again!" the man shrieked, "Tanks!" Major Mereeve cursed as he remembered just where those tanks had been built. The din of battle was growing and the outer perimeter was crumbling when the radio man finally regained contact with UNMEDF command on the Soviet aircraft carrier flagship sailing on the Mediterranean.

"This is Mereeve, in command of strike force Chubikoff, we need air strikes. We are being overrun by armor and infantry." The radio hissed a static filled sigh, then broke into a raspy voice.

"You must not let the target be recaptured — all is depending on you — all of the other objectives have been secured. The warheads must *not* be recaptured by the Syrians. Do you understand?" The attack was slowing as more Russians gave their lives in a vain attempt to stem the flow of tanks into the complex. It was apparent now to Major Mereeve that all was lost. Syrian tanks were everywhere in the small military base firing at buildings and hastily built earthworks — wherever they saw Russians giving resistance.

"This is strike force Chubikoff. We need a RED AIR STRIKE at target zero. I repeat, we need a RED AIR STRIKE at target zero. Am I understood?"

"Yes, Chubikoff, we understand — the Red Air Strike has been in readiness. We have been waiting only for your request. It is now on the way." Major Mereeve threw the microphone down and scrambled to the edge of the foxhole. Then he climbed out of the hole and ran to one of the larger buildings of the complex. There were men there firing their light weapons at tanks in an ineffective parody of defense.

"Get those bio-warheads up here!" Major Mereeve screamed above the deafening battle. "I want all those warheads out of that silo and to the surface in five minutes." The men ran to the rear of the shattered concrete room and called up the elevator. The first five of the twenty biologically lethal warheads came up from the subterranean storage silo and were rolled into the room.

"Hurry! There isn't much time left!" Mereeve looked out the broken window in time to see a Syrian tank burst into flames. "That's it, boys, just give us five more minutes — just five more minutes!" Another tank rounded the corner and a long tongue of flame streaked out to engulf the anti-tank crew that had destroyed the first tank. Russian paratroopers were throwing grenades at the flame throwing tank from the roof of a nearby building, but it rumbled through the miniature explosions seemingly unaffected by the blasts. Yet a few seconds later a tread leaped out from its rear and the huge monster stopped. Its turret turned slowly as if it were the head of the monster, turning to see where its assailants were hiding. Then an anti-tank missile shot forward and this tank also burst into flames. Men tried to escape fiery death, throwing the hatches open and skittering out onto the burning hull — only to meet the long frustrated fire of small arms.

While Major Mereeve had been turned toward the battle, the second set of five warheads had been brought up and the elevator, still working by some miracle of fate, had been sent back down for another load. When he turned back to the work he saw the third set of five appearing into the room. *Almost*, he thought, *almost.*

"Hurry there! Get them off the lift and send it back down!" He knew that it was only the bravery of the men outside that had kept the tanks away while they worked at bringing the warheads to the surface.

"The last load is on the way up, sir! Permission to go help outside?" the Sergeant who had been running the silo elevator asked. Major Mereeve knew how he felt — it would be much better to die fighting tanks on the small street.

"Permission granted, Sergeant." Without a word the man ran outside to help his comrades fight tanks that had been made in his own country. Major Mereeve turned back to the now almost empty room, he was kept company only by the twenty warheads they had come to destroy. Then the Red Air Strike arrived.

The mushroom cloud rose in the so typical fashion from the blast that destroyed all the Syrian tanks, all the Soviet paratroopers and most importantly, all the biological warheads.

Bradley had to get the desiccators to the other floors; one per floor with a small explosive charge under each. The charges would disperse the contents of the desiccators and provide enough heat to the catalyst to initiate the fusion reaction. He put one in the central hallway of each of the lower three laboratory levels and one in the spacious laboratory dining room on Level Three, just about in the center of the room. He wanted to place the last desiccator on Level Two — the level with barracks for the security forces. He wasn't going to initiate the reaction on the uppermost level because it was open to the outer atmosphere and he didn't want any unreacted material available for analysis later. He didn't want anyone else to know the mechanism of the laboratory's destruction.

As he approached the mutilated doorway between the dining area and the passage up to the security levels the stench of death grew stronger. He was tying a handkerchief around his face when Norton Richardson approached. Bradley hadn't seen the man since before Sally and he had started their search of the German's notes. The man had grown bent and slow. His face was heavily lined and huge dark sacks had appeared under his eyes. It appeared he had not slept a moment during their separation. He was worried and afraid; his hands trembled slightly and his eyes darted from Bradley's masked face to the knife on his hip then back again.

"Bradley, I'd like a few minutes please." Bradley didn't want to stop now that his work was almost finished, but the man was emphatic in his tone.

"Sure thing, Richardson, what can I do for you?" He pulled the bandana down from over his nose and mouth.

"Can we sit, please?" They walked a few feet to a table and chairs. Richardson offered a cigarette and they both smoked. "I want you to know that I understand your mission here. I've been trying to complete it in my mind but until an hour or so ago my prejudice had blinded me. Now I understand, and I'm ready for my . . . role in it. But not the girls Bradley, not my girls." He was begging and beginning to cry.

The darkness of the inorganic chemistry lab was back, blacker and thicker than before, oozing around and enveloping them in a cold, evil grip. Bradley wanted to comfort him, but Richardson cut him off before he could get out a word.

"I will stay Bradley, but not the girls. My wife is not a scientist, she knows nothing and Sally could never duplicate the work we did here alone. You've got to take them with you. I can't stand the thought of them dying. Their lives are the only reason I did the research here in the first place. You can't . . ." He broke into a fit of sobbing that overwhelmed his words, then sat whimpering with his head in his hands.

Then, for the first time, Bradley fully realized that the darkness was emanating from him, that his complete mission was to prevent the spread of the "selective genocide" secret, that he was expected to destroy the knowledge as well as the lab. His mind flew back to his conversation with Professor "Joe" Barkman. "It only takes one person to infect the entire world," he had said. And suddenly Bradley knew what Richardson knew — not only couldn't he let anyone out of the lab who had the attribute of carrying the disease, but he had to bury anyone with the knowledge of its engineering.

This time it was vectored toward the Jews but who would be next? Blacks? Whites? Orientals? The possibilities were endless. Bradley shuddered and slumped deeply into his chair as he accepted the need to bury the secret here, finally and irrevocably. He couldn't let

Richardson live to be forced to work on the project again; he couldn't let him work for America or even for the Bloc. His knowledge had to die and he knew it. It suddenly became clear to Bradley why he had been incapable of consummating a friendship with Sally. He had known then subconsciously what lay ahead.

"Sally knows, too, doesn't she?" Richardson's whimpering grew to unrestrained moaning. "Why did you let her work with you? Why didn't you keep her in the dark?" The older man was pulling at his hair and shaking his head as if a hot coal was burning within his skill.

"She can't do it alone, but they wouldn't make her do it alone. Don't you see? She could give them the key they need without doing any of the work herself." Bradley was berating him, but it was himself that he wanted to hurt. He didn't want to do what some computer had calculated he would do. He wanted to act humanly, to decide for himself his next actions, to resist the apparent predestination of his next steps. Only the Bloc had known him even more precisely than he had known himself. Bradley couldn't oppose actions that were the only ones possible for him to take. They had known that. They had set him up and there was nothing he could do about it. "Your wife is safe. You must find a way to make her leave with me." *And leave you and Sally here to die,* he thought. "I'm sorry, Richardson. I am truly sorry. I just don't have any choice." Richardson stood up and shuffled back from whence he came, even more bent and defeated than before. As he walked, Bradley could hear him moaning Sally's name over and over again.

radley carried the last desiccator up to the second level and placed it in the most central position he could find. The air was rank with decomposing bodies, as they had not cleared the top two floors of the effects of the Richardson's "No Alternative." He walked to the armory musing unhappily over the illogical life and death morals of war. Humans are a pretty callous species when they felt they were in the right. They found it supremely easy to kill each other if they could rationalize the act in any way. The people who ran the lab, the Bloc, the Richardsons and now Bradley himself, only worked from different rationalizations.

In the armory he found what he was looking for without any difficulty: Russian manufactured explosive charges with wind up timers. The charge was of a small yield but he didn't want too large an explosion — that might decompose the gigantic inorganic molecule that initiated the pseudo catalytic reaction. He placed the charge under the desiccator on Level Two without activating it, brought four more of the charges down to the lower levels and prepared them in the same way. He was still wondering how to get the elevator from Level Two to open once it reached the uppermost part of the complex.

On his way back up to the elevator in question, Sally Richardson intercepted him crossing the research dining room.

"You're some kind of asshole aren't you? My father's an emotional wreck — you didn't have to torture him before you murdered him did you?" She knew! She had known where events were going and she hadn't been upset until her father broke down. Bradley stammered when he tried to speak.

"I didn't want to hurt him, Sally. I was upset with this whole dirty play and my anger broke on him. I'm sorry . . . so terribly sorry for everything." She was granite. Her face was thoughtful, yet unafraid. He envied her strength. "You know I can only take your mother out with me."

"I should have let you die with the rest of them. We should have stepped over your body and made a run for it on our own, but at first I thought you had come only to take us out of here." She choked out an unamused, dry laugh that made Bradley feel even filthier. "Then I thought I could help you, get to know you so you wouldn't be able to finish what you had been sent here to do. But I realized when we were in my room that you are an emotional retard — empty of any compassion or love. Still I hoped you would let it come as a surprise to them, let it be over before they realized what was happening, but you didn't even have enough mercy to let it come easy. You had to taunt him with it. He tried to keep me out of the research, you know. He begged me, he ordered me, he did everything but tie me up in my room. It wasn't his fault that I wouldn't listen, it was mine. I was ready to pay the price for my mistake but I wasn't prepared to see my father driven into catatonic regression by a sadist."

"Sally, I . . ."

"Go on, finish what you came to do. I know now that's the only thing of importance to you." She turned and walked a few brisk strides then spun wildly around. "And you don't have to worry about taking my mother with you. She'll never leave him now!" Her face was no longer buttressed against her anguish. It was running with her tears as she turned and sprinted away.

After setting the Russian timers for twenty minutes, Bradley had left the lab without saying goodbye to the ones he was killing. The elevator from Level Two to Level One had been relatively easy to short out so it would travel with the door still open. He had run through the upper security level carrying an AK-47, not knowing what to expect upon his return to the surface three days after his entrance. As he had approached the door, some small carnivore dropped an unrecognizable chunk of flesh across the threshold before scurrying out through the tangled doorway.

Bradley wondered why no one had come to check the silence of the laboratory as he climbed back to the rim of the valley. He supposed something else very important must have distracted their attention; maybe another Bloc target had been hit in a spectacular manner.

He stopped climbing at the rim and sat behind a rock to await the final act of the play. Then, just when he had decided something had gone wrong, he felt the ground shake and instants later heard the dull crump that telegraphed success. The valley wavered for long rumbling moments then the ground expanded into a transient mountain before collapsing back into a large depression. He knew it was all gone: the lab, the rooms, the different levels, the equipment, the bodies, the biological weapons, the Richardsons — all devoured by the searing heat of the nuclear explosion. He turned away and began the trek back to civilization, his physical burden much lighter than the weight he had packed in three days before.

Walking across the Libyan desert alone, toward his prearranged pick up point, he had only his thoughts for company. The Richardsons had been fine compassionate, respected people. They had been jerked out of their old lives by powers they couldn't understand and had no chance to resist. They had been manipulated into a situation where their survival depended on their actions. Actions they made without prior intent or malice; actions that once taken, however innocently, however reluctantly, preordained their final hapless encounter with another incomprehensible power. He felt a kinship with them, a helpless ineffectual feeling of being manipulated.

Bradley reached the rendezvous point without mishap two hours before the nightly fly by. He wondered if they would even bother to pick him up and hoped his usefulness had been expended. But the jet flew by in a dangerously low scream and acknowledged his signal light with a blink of its landing beacon. Forty minutes later he was boarding the Soviet built and manned helicopter that took him away from Libya and out to the nervous men waiting for him on the Mediterranean.

General Silas Riley knew how important a precise timetable was to the fulfillment of the Bloc's plan. He knew the targets must be taken in lightning strikes across a huge area. He knew and depended on the crucial need to dismantle or otherwise neutralize these targets in the least possible time. He knew the importance to Bloc conspirators a quick relinquishing of captured terrain, material and personnel would hold in the inevitable piracy trials to come. He knew the necessity of a passive surrender to the proper world authorities once these things had been accomplished. He knew that each minute's delay would bring the jaws of a world military machine closer to the now fully exposed Bloc confederacy. Most importantly of all, with the reception of the radio dispatch he crumpled with a victorious smile, he knew that all the Bloc objectives had, with varying degrees of difficulty, been achieved. Now his own private timetable could begin. He turned to the radioman as he pulled the carefully written message from his breast pocket.

"Send this one back Sergeant; I already have it coded." He waited in the room until the message was sent, then recovered its possession. He was self congratulatory as he strode out of the hastily set up radio room. He had all the cards and had just played his ace. Shortly, he

would be a very, very rich man, quietly retired in Argentina. And if
the Bloc was quick in realizing he had them, their plan wouldn't suf-
fer much at all. The Bloc would be poorer, that's all . . . much, much
poorer.

J erusalem: IBS wire system

A sudden war wages over this entire portion of the world, yet until this morning this city had seemed divorced from the violence. At dawn, massive explosions shook those of us living here from our sleep, bringing the incomprehensible strife yet another step closer to us. Gigantic columns of black smoke billowed from the portion of the city long called the Mount of Olives. From my hotel room, one could watch the unwarranted attacks of war planes upon the defenseless shrines that have stood above this city for centuries. In minutes it was over. The attackers were gone before the first Israeli fighter planes appeared, but Israeli officials state that all the attacking warplanes were destroyed as they fled. It is not clear how the extensive Israeli early alert system was breached, but the official explanation is computer error. The attackers have yet to be denounced as indeed the enemy being fought in most of the countries of the Middle East arena has still not been officially identified. However, sources in the military claim the United Nations peace keeping forces are responsible.

In other action . . .

The United Nations had for two days been a madhouse of frenzied yet ineffectual activity. The Security Council had been in constant meeting since the first reports of warfare in the Middle East had stunned the world. The General Assembly had met in the dead of night when the Security Council announced that the UNMEDF had not taken, and was not at the time taking, any orders from them.

There were proposals for a new U.N. force to rush to the area to vanquish the first — but somehow none of the countries involved wanted anything more to do with United Nations forces. Ambassador Stone had been in seclusion until the messenger came to his door with a one line message: "Only the Riley problem remains — begin our plea."

Stone's wife watched him as he crumpled the note, tossed it into the fireplace and then waited to see that it burned. A log rolled out, pushing against the grill. Stone seemed not to notice as he turned to his wife.

"I'll be going into the city, now."

She had felt his anguish the past few days but had known that he could not share his pain. Now she felt that everything was at last coming to the surface.

"Robert, what is it? Do you know anything about the U.N. forces . . . it was your proposal." He smiled an unhappy, yet loving, half smile at his good wife who always knew when and what to ask.

"Yes, it was my proposal . . . in part." A short, thoughtful pause then with another little smile, "Watch the television, sweetheart. Everything will be on the television very shortly."

Stone's arrival at the Security Council chamber caused a rationalizing quiet to fall over the previously irrational rantings and accusations that had prospered. He was given the floor immediately, almost before he had gotten to his deputy who had bravely weathered the storm until his arrival.

"Gentlemen, you have many questions to which you feel I have the answers . . . in this you are quite correct." The chamber erupted as ambassadors from the West gasped; from the East flared in anger. "But first let me clarify one point." Stone reached forward to the nameplate that read "United States," picked it up and handed it to his deputy. He recovered another placard from his briefcase and placed in front of him, "Independent."

"I speak for no country, just as the men so bravely sacrificing their lives in the Middle East fight for no country. Although we come from many nations, we reject any national allegiances. We ally ourselves only with humanity and the prevention of world destruction by man. Some good leaders of the Middle Eastern countries involved have been earnestly pursuing peace, both publicly and privately. Our only goal has been the prevention of the Armageddon that would result if these earnest attempts proved futile. Since these good men's words have failed, we were forced to act! We have acted at this moment, for the good of the countries involved, for the good of the world, also so intimately involved, for the good of millions yet unborn.

"We have seized and destroyed all nuclear, chemical and biological weaponry that previously existed, so perilously, in the fragile Middle Eastern equilibrium. The danger of a cancerous nuclear and biological battle spreading into the rest of the world has been neutralized." At this moment a messenger, the same one that had come to his home that morning, gave Stone another note.

"Excuse me," as Stone read a slight murmur rustled through the chamber. Stone finished the message, then with a somewhat more saddened face, continued. He seemed to direct every word to the Soviet contingency. "As you all know, most of our objectives were secured within hours of the initial movements. Only in one spot has the objective failed to be secured. This objective was a biological warhead storage silo in Syria. The warheads stored in this complex could, if improperly used, destroy life on one third of our planet." More horrified gasps. "A unit of very brave, highly trained, paratroopers was dropped into the area to secure the complex and destroy forever the bio-warheads in the vortex of a small nuclear explosion." The words seemed to radiate sorrow to the Soviet representatives.

"These paratroopers had once been Soviet nationals before their honor forced them to join us in our task. Unfortunately, they received extremely heavy resistance at the warhead storage facility. They were attacked by Syrian armored forces almost immediately upon their arrival. Last night they were overrun and the horrifying warheads were in danger of being recaptured. The brave men of this group of 'Bloc' sympathizers brought the warheads out of their protective underground silo, and then called in a nuclear strike on their own positions. Only their bravery and sacrifice made their mission a success. The tremendously lethal biological weapons have all been destroyed.

"The world will long remember these soldiers as men who valued the lives of their fellow men above their own." Stone lowered his head and the chamber was quiet for long moments. Then with a quick restart, Stone renewed his explanation. "Now all the dangerous weapons have been wrenched from the antagonist's hands. It remains up to the legitimate United Nations to prevent the conventional war brewing, but we of this 'pirate political Bloc' have prevented a nuclear-biological slaughter. We await any tribunal you may decide to organize to present a more detailed defense of our actions."

Stone quickly stepped out of the chamber before the flood of questions would prevent him from making his departure.

The first thing Bradley noticed about the fleet was its swollen size. Where three days before a small carrier task force had sailed, a huge fleet of ships steamed. He counted two more carriers and their support ships plus other large ships that were unidentifiable to his untrained eye. The helicopter flew into the center of the fleet, escorted by a flight of Migs. When it landed the jets rolled up and away to assume a circular path around the ship. Bradley was snatched from the helicopter by two Soviet officers immediately after touching down and whisked up to the bridge where Captain Beilikov paced anxiously. Upon Bradley's arrival he stepped toward the doorway, as if they would leave the bridge together immediately, then abruptly spun back to his second in command. They exchanged a few short words, obviously, even to Bradley, words without any extraneous felicities. Beilikov nodded then swiftly turned back to his new passenger.

"Come, Bradley, there is no time. Things have gone badly." They left the bridge and headed down the familiar corridor that led to the captain's quarters.

"What happened? The lab is gone!" Bradley added the last in a sudden wave of doubt that was vocalized as a challenge.

"Not here, Bradley . . . let us wait until we reach my cabin, please." The walk seemed longer to Bradley than during his first visit but they soon arrived, Bradley's exhausted legs protesting at the swift gait. Once again, Beilikov took to the less comfortable desk chair and Bradley poured himself into the Russian's caressingly deep-tufted recliner. Bradley noticed for the first time that Beilikov's eyes were angry and to his sick surprise, he appeared to be angry at him.

"One of your capitalistic brothers has become a pirate even to us, Bradley. He has taken a nuclear missile silo and reprogrammed the computers for new targets. Seven major cities are within the strike radius of his missiles." He stopped and looked at Bradley as though he wanted to add: 'What do you think of yourself now, capitalistic dog?'

"Hey wait a minute. People are people. Someone *had* to flip out in a thing like this." Bradley stopped what he had planned on being a long convincing, calming explanation when Beilikov cocked his head in confusion.

"Flip out. What is this?"

"Lose control, become illogical, go insane." The captain's eyes softened a little, and he leaned back in the swivel chair, rubbing his reddened eyes as if he had been missing out on a lot of sleep. "Yes . . . insane . . . but not so illogical, I'm afraid."

"Why don't you fill me in Captain? We really can't discuss this if only one of us knows what we're talking about."

"The American General Riley was to secure the nuclear missile base in the southern Israeli desert. The warheads were to have been removed from the area and turned over to the United Nations during our public plea for leniency. He sent us the safety canisters with dummy warheads, then retargeted the missiles. He then sent a radio message stating a demand for money. All the money we have earmarked for legal defense and family support. He threatens to start launching missiles if we don't comply."

He waited for opinions or questions, but Bradley had none. His mind was back on an airplane reading a dossier explaining "the 66.67% probability of betrayal." Back listening to the old man from the desert tell him why he would do even the dirtiest job for the Bloc . . . even assassination. Then his memory brought him back to the car ride with Samuel and their conversation.

160

"What the hell is all this assassination bullshit?" he had demanded. He remembered how Samuel had explained away this part of his training almost too easily. Then he had finished up with, "you will, of course, decide prior to the event."

"Are you listening to me, Bradley? This is very important." Captain Beilikov's voice brought him back to the cabin, the ship and the reality of the present. He realized he could expect to be asked the big favor pretty damn soon.

"Yes, I'm listening to you, Captain. I was just thinking about some special training they gave me that I didn't understand at the time, but I think I do now."

"Then you know that you are to kill him?"

"No . . . I suspected that I would be asked to do so."

"There is a man on his way here from Italy. He is to be the one to ask you, I think."

"Is it Samuel?"

"I was not informed of the man's identity, Bradley."

"No . . . he's very careful about that. Do you know any details of how it is to be done?"

"I have told you all I know, except . . ." Bradley encouraged him to continue with his eyes and with his continued silence. "Except that Riley is in command of an armored division entrenched around a reinforced concrete, subterranean silo containing at least six nuclear weapons, maybe more. I don't believe he can be reached for assassination.

"Well, it's like I said before, they seem to know what they're doing. After all, Captain, you didn't think I could neutralize the lab."

"I hope that I am wrong once again." His mood changed, he shifted in his chair to gain a more comfortable position then pulled open his lower desk drawer. Out came a bottle of scotch and two glasses. "I find that there are a few things the West does well Bradley. Scotch is one of them." During the several drinks of warm straight scotch, Captain Beilikov told Bradley of the fiasco in Syria. He seemed extremely bitter that Bloc intelligence had not known of the Syrian armor in the vicinity of the paratroop drop. "It is a very hard thing to order the death of so many of one's own people, Bradley. A very hard thing to do because of bad luck."

"Yes, I know Captain, but it wouldn't be any easier if there had only been a few of them, would it?" Bradley was thinking about the Richardsons.

"One would be too many, Bradley. Too many indeed."

Bradley decided to get drunk, but Beilikov went back to his bridge. Even a few unnecessary moments away from his now encircled ships caused him much guilt. His return to duty ruined Bradley's taste for getting drunk. He fell asleep in the chair instead.

As comfortable as the soft recliner was, he awakened to cramped joints and knotted muscles. His first thought was to move to the Russian's bunk, but with sleep-delayed clarity of mind, he stood and stretched his misused body. His stomach growled insistently as he carefully popped the vertebrae of his spine. He had slept six hours and had his nerves not been tingling from anticipation, he probably could have slept ten or twelve more.

Outside the captain's cabin he was greeted in Russian by a waiting sailor who motioned for him to follow. It wasn't a long walk, but long enough to disorient him. The many turns and stairways leading from steel gray corridors to other apparently identical passageways seemed indistinguishable from one another. They arrived at the small blank-walled room that served as Senior Officer's mess after a final turn in the route his guide had chosen. Samuel sat at the metal table studying a thick document through semicircular reading glasses he wore far down on his nose. He glanced over their tops when he heard Bradley come in, rearranged the pages of the report, placed it into his briefcase and rising, removed the little bankeresque glasses.

A few short words in Russian and the escorting sailor disappeared.

"I didn't know you spoke Russian, Samuel."

"Yes, a little. I've learned not to over brief people about myself. It keeps things . . ."

"Safe?"

"Uncomplicated. I'd like to take this moment to congratulate you on the success of your trip to Libya. It was a uniquely smooth operation."

"Turned out just like you expected, didn't it?"

"Very similar, indeed . . . but the laboratories annihilation was even more than we expected."

"You can say that again!" It was the sandy voice of Bradley's trainer almost yelling as he strode into the room. He wore Russian fatigues without insignia, his head shining in the bright light. "Have you showed him the aerials yet? Boy, you sure kicked their butt down there in Libya. We got some aerial photos that'll take your breath away. Biggest damn crater I ever saw. What you use anyway, boy?" This was the question Bradley knew he had to avoid answering.

"Listen, that's over. I don't want to talk about it . . . or the Richardsons. If all you want to do is Monday morning quarterback, I'm going. But I was under the impression that you had something to ask me to do."

"No, Michael, we don't have to talk about the Libyan matter now." Samuel's voice held a faint shading of uncertainty as he changed the subject. "You know that we are here because of General Riley's little gambit?"

"I know he has half a dozen nuclear weapons held to your head." Bradley was enjoying making Samuel uncomfortable by translating his antiseptic vagueness into infected reality.

"Quite right. At any rate we have a plan to neutralize his check and end the game by placing him in check mate." He stubbornly refused to abandon the chess analogy.

"You want me to kill him, isn't that what you're trying to say?" His eyes remained blank as if he hadn't heard.

"Our information suggests that Riley is most probably not operating with the full support of his troops. They probably still think they are doing what the Bloc directs Riley to do. If we could relieve Riley of command . . ."

"You mean, kill him, don't you Samuel?"

"Yes . . . I mean kill him, Michael." There, he had forced him to dirty his hands. It made Bradley feel good to have made Samuel admit his murderous position.

"Boy, you should see the weapon system I got for you. You'll be so far away from the guy, it'll be like sending him a message through the mail. Yeah, Air Mail." The old man was so pleased with his comparison he broke into loud gravelly laughter. "Come on, boy, I got it down the hall. Wait till you see it, positively a work of art. Won't take you but a minute to learn how to use it either." When Bradley reached the door after the old man, he turned to where Samuel sat watching.

"I'll kill him, Samuel. Just like you knew I would, but this is it — the end — fini — no more. I'm out after this, do you understand?"

"Yes, Michael, I understand. Good luck." Bradley followed the old man out of the room wondering how much Samuel understood.

The weapon was heavy and awkwardly large; even in its disassembled state it didn't pack well. The weight was constantly shifting on Bradley's back, causing him to stumble often as he crossed the rocky terrain. The hike was necessarily long as there was a high probability that General Riley expected the Bloc to try some such preventative move before paying his outlandish ransom demand.

He reached the rise in the landscape that was his destination in the late morning, before the relentless sun grew to its full intensity. From the top of the rise he could see the installation's surface refinements almost two miles away. He lunched on protein bars and warm water before unpacking the weapon.

It was a rifle, yet it resembled one only distantly. The non-reflective barrel was far too long and the hollow stock was bloated and misshapened to increase its volume. He filled the stock with sand for added weight. It stood massively on a low tripod that he had staked firmly to the ground, a giant cylindrically shaped scope and range finder package road piggyback down two thirds of its length. He sighted the direction with the scope and dialed in the elevation required from the range finder's electronic printout. Then he activated his signal beacon. He was ready.

In the middle afternoon the motivational stimulus arrived. Bradley had only been told that after his signal some event would cause Riley to briefly venture from his underground invulnerability. They came over the horizon, flying close formation, yet looking insect-like in the distance. He counted nine as they grew close enough for armored vehicles to begin firing at them. The gunships returned fire with waves of rockets and streams of tracers. They landed among the tanks and stubby concrete structures, quickly spilling out their pas-sengers before leaping back into the air to give covering fire. One of the helicopters exploded and crashed as men began running from out of the blockhouse entrance of the site.

The airborne troops were attempting to plant charges on the immense platform door of the silo, but this required they attack across open ground under the guns of tanks and infantry. More troops flowed from the blockhouse and the clatter of gunfire redoubled. Surface to air missiles began zipping into the buzzing sky and several more helicopters fell into flaming explosions. At the compound the invaders made another feeble rush across the exposed surface of the silo doorway but were driven back into slightly less exposed positions.

The last airship crashed into the concrete door of the silo without effect and the surviving paratroopers began throwing their weapons down in an attempt at surrender. The first few were killed in the heat of battle so quickly finished, but suddenly the firing subsided and the defenders walked openly to their prisoners. Then there appeared to be some confusion while they herded the beaten men into a line to be searched. Bradley realized that the airborne troops must have been Americans as well, possibly men who were known to the victors as Bloc members. The confusion seemed to explode into a heated debate with arms pointing to the blockhouse. Bradley loaded the absurdly large cartridge into the weapon and brought the sight to the group of men, checking the range finder to be sure of barrel elevation.

Two men appeared at the door of the blockhouse and began walking across the littered compound toward the cross hairs of the scope. Bradley identified General Riley and his aide from the photos he had studied during his briefing. They walked briskly toward the ensuing argument. Some of the prisoners pointed accusing fingers in his direction and the general broke into a run, his arms flailing. He finally stopped close to the captors and pointed to the unarmed men with unmistakable meaning. Bradley slowly spun a wheel on the side of the tripod mounting and the crosshair moved smoothly to Riley's upper chest. One or two of the captors raised their weapons a little but appeared reluctant to coldly kill other unarmed Americans. Americans who had probably been trying to convince them they were loyal Bloc military men sent to stop Riley from launching nuclear weapons toward innocent cities.

Riley lurched to one of the men and wrenched his machine gun from him. As he turned the gun toward the prisoners, Bradley's hand spun the wheel, keeping the thin crosshairs on his target's upper torso. Riley raised the machine gun to his hip and Bradley squeezed off the only round in the weapon. There was no recoil of the massive assembly and Bradley saw Riley clearly when the shot clubbed him viciously to the ground. The men, both captives and captors, looked stupidly down at him, unable to comprehend what had happened. Then with the lazily rolling in of the sound of the shot, they looked up and around them. Bradley hit his signal beacon again and waited as medics rushed to the fallen general's side.

Bradley could see the renewed energy of the prisoner's explanations and within minutes the sky was crowded with more gunships. They landed anywhere there was room, unloaded troops and flew off to make room for others to land. There was no shooting this time. Bradley abandoned the weapon and lit a cigarette as he walked down the slope toward the compound.

Captain Beilikov watched the helicopter carrying his new friend, Michael Bradley, lift away from the flight deck, turn slowly, then blast off northward in a storm of blade and jet blast. He stood watching as it gradually faded into the wispy white clouds, thinking how alike they were beyond their obvious minor differences and how neither of their lives would ever be what they once were. Only when it was completely gone from his sight did he begin the walk to his quarters.

He felt the many eyes of dependent crew members following him as he trudged alone across the steel flight deck. He knew they were waiting for some encouraging speech or congratulatory announcement now that they had finished what they had been working on for so long. Yet he felt empty and alone, even among the thousands of men at his side. A strong wind was blowing from the East, and the ship drove westerly with the wind washing across her stern. It seemed unnatural to him to have it such with none of his planes in flight to watch over and protect the ship. Yet they were captives now and hadn't the need for defensive considerations. His small task force was tightly encircled and closely watched by the larger, infinitely more powerful fleet that convoyed them to their Security Council designated destination of Marseilles. He was glad that they had not been boarded as the Soviet Union had at first demanded. He needed this last short cruise with his men and his ship unmolested on the smaller scale, even if prisoners in the larger frame of reality. He wondered about the fate of the men he commanded once they disembarked at Marseilles and were taken into international custody. He hoped a tolerant, understanding world would handle their disposition honorably.

The familiar corridors and passageways on his side trip to the bridge beckoned to him in a mute attempt at communication. He held onto handrails unnecessarily, to feel the touch of his lover in their last time together. Once on the bridge, he never assumed command of the ship, only observed silently that all was as it should be now that the end was near. He nodded his approval to the officers present then continued his silent walk to his quarters.

The Lewis Carroll book the American had been reading such a distant short span of time ago caught his eye from the confusion on his desk. As he sat slowly into his black reclining chair, he shook his head with a cynical smile, thinking he had never really understood much of the story. He bent forward to reach the American service pistol cached under the chair. He pulled the weapon from the leather case and checked the operation of his heavy, yet precision made works.

"Only on our mutual enemies, Bradley . . . Only on our mutual enemies." He spoke the last as if there was someone else in the cabin with him and hearing his voice he looked around as if expecting it to be true. But he was quite alone when he put the barrel of the gun in his mouth and loudly ended his life.

B radley was sitting in a small fold down seat when the helicopter left Captain Beilikov's flagship. He was uncomfortable
because his clothing didn't match the utilitarian interior of a
machine of war. He couldn't relax and lean back against the white
painted metal for fear of soiling the light brown, three-piece suit the
Bloc, probably Samuel he thought, had sent for him to wear. The suit
was Italian and fit immaculately across his hard-to-fit shoulders without bulging at the waist. A few months before he would have been
surprised, but he had grown accustomed to the Bloc's awareness of
detail. An awareness of detail that contradicted the fact that over
four hundred Russian paratroopers had been vaporized because of a
mistake in planning; the first mistake he had noticed in an otherwise
flawless operation. It made him wonder if it had been a mistake at
all. Maybe they had known they were dropping the Russians into an
armor staging area; maybe they just didn't wait until the armor had
left because they knew what action the Russian commander would
take when the recapture of the warheads was imminent. Bradley cut
off his distasteful mental ramblings with one last vocalized thought,
"They know too damn much about how we're going to react." The
noise of the engines engulfed his voice, making it silent even to him.

The helicopter landed on a privately owned yacht from which he was ferried to shore and a waiting car. A private plane shuttled him to Rome where he took a commercial flight out of Europe. He was afraid the red carpet treatment meant being put on the shelf amiably until they had some future need of his talents. The thought ruined a surprisingly good in-flight meal, although by the time it was served he was famished.

In New York he was met by a pleasant woman in an expensive pantsuit. She had a ticket for San Francisco, but asked if indeed that was where he wanted to go. She also had a ticket for Los Angeles. Bradley took the next flight for San Francisco and Sharon.

Flying into a major city on an overcast night is a little like waking up to discover the first snow of winter. It is an expected moment, if not mundane; yet it possesses some subtle power to quicken the pulse during the initial awareness of expectations fulfilled. In this transient instant of transition from mental anticipation to physical existence, a fleeting perception of stupefaction arises. Such was Bradley's arrival through the cloud cover into the sight of the lights of San Francisco. He had known the time was coming, but it seemed to arrive too soon. Though he had rehearsed the reunion a thousand silently glib times, he had nothing ready to say to Sharon when they met.

Bradley was the last off the plane and the least impatient to claim his luggage. He thought about renting a car but realized Sharon probably had his car at her folks' place. He took a cab into town. It was a long drive but he still had a pocket full of the money given him in Rome. He decided on a nice motel near the wharf where Sharon and he had stayed several times before. It was close to good sea food and a trolley ride away from downtown, but not so extravagant that he'd have to explain his windfall to Sharon.

He called room service for a bottle of scotch and some ice before getting into the shower. It was midnight and several stiff drinks before he had the operator get him an outside line. The phone rang so many times that everyone in Sharon's place must have already been asleep. Long seconds after the ringing stopped Sharon's sleepy voice came on the line.

"Hello?"

"How are you, Share?"

"Oh, Mickey. I've been so worried. Your last call was so strange. I mean you didn't sound like yourself. Are you all right? Where are you? When are you coming home?"

"I'm in town . . . in the motel down by the wharf. Would you meet me somewhere? I'd like to see you."

"I'll be right there!" The receiver banged as if she had just let it drop. Bradley could hear activity in the background, then Sharon's mother telling her to calm down. The receiver was once again lifted and Mrs. Klein was on the other end.

"Sharon's a little excited, Michael, but she should be back downstairs soon." Bradley heard Sharon yell from far off. "She says to tell you she'll be on the road in five minutes, but she just jumped into the shower — better make it fifteen. Never seen her move so fast before."

"Well, OK. She knows where I am. Tell her I'll be waiting. Thanks a lot, Mrs. Klein, I'll see you soon."

"All right, Michael, I'll pass it on to her . . . I'm glad you're well. Everyone was worried."

"Well, I'm sure everything will be all right now." Bradley was beginning to run out of logical reassurances. They had the common problem of expecting more words before they hung up and moments of awkward silence followed.

"Yes, well I'll go hurry her along, good bye."

"Goodbye, thanks again." Bradley ended the stumbling telephone conversation with a subconscious sensation of gratitude. He mixed himself another drink then turned on the television. A special news program was trying to unravel the recent startling events in the Mideast and United Nations.

"With the ratification of the joint U.S.—Soviet resolution the controversial question of jurisdiction over the raiders has been answered. Amid boisterous objections of Third World representatives, the Security Council announced that since the greatest proportion of the men involved were under oath to the United Nations as military personnel, the U.N. has first and final authority over the disposition of their cases. The U.N. will also pay war reparations for damages caused by forces admitted to sovereign nations under the protection of the United Nations flag. No details of how or where these funds are to be raised were announced."

Bradley realized that this was a very good thing for the Bloc's now docile warriors. An international court would be exceedingly more receptive to a defense that depended upon proving their actions were a necessity than separate courts within the individual nations. It was also obvious to him, by the speed with which the USA and USSR had pushed through their resolution, that they were not entirely unhappy with the events that had reduced the likelihood of a nuclear or biological encounter involving them.

"World Health Organization scientists today confirmed Syrian claims that a nuclear weapon was used against Syrian troops on Syrian soil. Their report read, in part, 'The device was of very low yield and was exceptionally clean in nature. Effects of the detonation are localized to a small area with minimal radiation levels for an explosive device of this kind.' IBC science advisors tell us that a nuclear weapon with such relatively low residual radiation levels is deliberately manufactured for what the WHO report calls cleanliness or low radiation yield. The WHO report also noted that warhead remnants found in the wreckage of the missile silo were identified as being capable of carrying biologically lethal payloads. This agrees with Ambassador Stone's preliminary announcement to the General Assembly and the more detailed account given in the recent Bloc Communiqué, which stated that the nuclear device was used only when conventional methods for the destruction of the biological weapons had failed."

This was too much. Bradley drained his drink, then got up and switched the tube off. The news account was far too biased. He could see that the Bloc was already influencing the world opinion on which they were so dependent. He wondered at the breadth and extent of Bloc influence. It would take a mammoth amount of pull to shade the news released by the International Broadcasting System.

He called room service for more ice after mixing some scotch with a little of the cold water left in the ice bucket. He had just reclined into the pillows he had piled against the bed board when there was a knock on the door. Reaching for his wallet, he rose to answer.

"That was fast," he said as he opened the door.

"World's record!" All his thoughts of room service left with the surprise of seeing Sharon again. She took the half step across to him, her purse falling to the floor as she reached out. His move toward her caused them to meet on the threshold of the room. Her arms circled around his chest as he engulfed her shoulders with his own. They held on to each other with the vice-like, motionless grip of emotions more irresistible than any associated with carnal attraction. Wordlessly they stood in the doorway squeezing each other in a desperate attempt to bring themselves closer. He crushed her richly fragrant, caressingly soft hair against his downturned face. Aching from the hot, then cold, dampness of her eyes on his neck there was no time, only the timeless instant of reunion. There was no ardor, only the immense need to be close and the frustrating impossibility of growing any nearer. Sharon began to shake and the dampness on Bradley's neck became icy rivulets that flowed under his collar and down his chest. The wallet he had been holding against her fell when he raised his hand to stroke her hair.

"It's all right, Sharon. Everything is OK now."

"I know . . . this is terrible of me. I didn't want to make a scene. I was afraid that I had lost you, but you're back now. I'm being silly, I guess. It was just so strange the way you suddenly left. I still don't understand." As she spoke, the trembling slowed and the crying subsided into occasional sniffles. They were still half way outside the room, tightly embraced when Bradley's order from room service arrived.

The waiter was a teenaged black kid with a red jacket and bow tie. His eyes slid slowly up Sharon's long legs to linger on her behind before continuing upward to her long straight, black hair. He saw that Bradley had noticed his inventory and spoke bitterly before coming closer.

"Room service."

Sharon jerked with a start and released her grasp slightly. Bradley unwound his arms and stepped back until Sharon reluctantly let go completely. The waiter eyed her breasts through the thin white blouse she wore. It was the first moment Bradley had noticed how enticingly she was dressed and how perfectly she was made up. He really couldn't blame the waiter for looking, but his pulse was beginning to beat in his temples.

"How much?" He moved Sharon a little into the room with the pressure of his hands on her shoulders and then bent to recover both his wallet and her purse.

"One seventy-five," the waiter spoke while he was still bent over. Bradley handed the purse to Sharon and took a twenty from his wallet.

"A dollar seventy five for that little bit of ice," Sharon complained. "You've got to be crazy!" She was back in the doorway looking around Bradley's shoulder, speaking in a comically indignant manner. The waiter was smirking as he waited, the tray in one hand and the check in the other. Bradley held the bill up to him without helping out with the tray. For a moment the kid didn't know what to do. Finally he took the money with the hand already holding the check. Bradley pulled the bucket of ice off the tray and handed it back to Sharon.

"You can sign for this, *sir.*" The '*sir*' was intentionally inflected to show his distaste in saying it. "This way I'll have to come back upstairs with your change, *sir.*" He pronounced the '*sir*' almost tauntingly. Bradley felt the anger pumping from the recently uncapped well of violence the Bloc had known to be waiting dormant within him. So long dormant, yet so deftly activated into boiling malignance that it knotted muscles and constricted capillaries infinitely faster than reason could be applied. A reservoir of psychopathic violence subtly released internally by the bombardment of external stimuli to which he would otherwise never have been exposed.

The young waiter's face changed from arrogance to confusion when he saw the violence in Bradley's eyes. Then when he noticed Bradley's rigid stance, his expression transformed to the wary fear of one dealing with a rabid dog. He stepped backward a step, afraid to speak, afraid to leave. The rage within Bradley was at a constant maximum, poised for an instant before translation into action, yet the moment lengthened.

"Mickey?" and with the timid sound of Sharon's voice the moment had passed. The over distended fury collapsed back into the fiery wellhead and was extinguished by lack of fuel.

Bradley's muscles began to relax with the exhalation of a long, hot breath. The young room service waiter watched him warily, his earlier contempt replaced with caution.

"Keep the change, kid." The waiter stood staring blindly as if he didn't comprehend. "Go on. Everything is all right." The teenager turned to walk away, looking back with his face coming to rest on his shoulder, continuing to stare while with unsteady strides he moved off down the hallway. He broke into a clumsy run toward the end of the corridor, still looking over his shoulder as he went around the corner.

After Bradley closed the door behind him, he saw that Sharon was worried.

"Are you OK, Mickey? Is everything really all right?"

"Yes, Sharon, I'm fine now. I feel better than I have in some time." He took her into his arms again.

"But God, Mickey, an eighteen dollar tip?"

"Eighteen dollars and twenty five cents, and worth every penny too. You tip for service and believe me he just performed one hell of a service."

For the first time in months, they kissed. It began almost hastily, as though the time had come for them to kiss passionately and any delay would risk magnifying their sexual unfamiliarity, as if any postponement of the moment would make the kiss more awkward. But with the softness of her body and the eagerness of her lips and tongue, Bradley felt the discomfort fleeing before a wave of excitement. His body rose instinctively to a state of sexual readiness and the increased energy of Sharon's kiss revealed that she had felt the change through their clothing. His hands dropped to her small, well defined hips, exploring their width, cupping the full softness from underneath as she began to rub rhythmically against his excitement now large between them. Then the exploring hands, Bradley's hands, were under the filmy blouse, stroking the velvety skin of her lower back. A whimper rose from somewhere deep inside her and her moist mouth pressed hard against his own. His hands continued up her spine in their survey of the perfectly smooth skin, now warm under a cool wet film of perspiration. One of her hands pressed to gain entrance between their two close bodies. Then her hand was on him, rubbing, clutching, driving him forward.

He felt himself rapidly approaching the limit of his sensitivity, racing to the instant of commitment. He began to pull away, he didn't want it to happen this way. He needed desperately to be in control of himself. Sharon's almost violent kiss continued as she moaned a negative grunt to his pushing back and away from her. She increased the speed and intensity with which she rubbed herself against him. And with the explosion that came from within him, he had an instantaneous vision of hurricane force winds blasting down laboratory halls, screeching as they carried everything in their path from the searing vortex of explosion, of concrete walls collapsing as if canvas flats in some obscene play, imploding as the irresistible power of immensely high temperatures and pressures raced through the complex, of Sally Richardson hurtling down a passageway, tumbling end over end, a silent scream on her lips as she was consumed by the inferno.

Bradley's body was stiff with terror before the last automatic spasms of climax had ended. Each breath seemed to need individual attention in order to be drawn. Sharon had released him when she had felt the unmistakable signs of orgasm. She became for Bradley a barely recognizable image at the end of a long dark tube.

"I'm sorry, Mickey . . . I just lost control, I guess." Her image became larger as if he were traveling down the tube to the end at which she waited.

"No." The tube blinked out of existence. "No . . . it was me. I lost control . . . but for a moment I thought I had it back."

New York — UPI

Secretary General Mario Putchini announced today that the United Nations Security Council would prosecute the Middle East pirates before the full General Assembly who will assume the responsibility of judgment. Putchini, a past President of the European Economic Community, outlined the plan during a speech broadcast live by satellite to five continents. The procedure, which shows many similarities to the U.S. impeachment process, will be aided by the unlimited use of the sophisticated computer system of the E.E.C. located in Rome. All appeals will be taken to the International Court of Justice in The Hague, the Netherlands.

Already it has been decided by the General Assembly that the military prisoners being held in camps in southern France will be afforded full rights of prisoners of war as stipulated by the conference of Geneva. Special attention will be given to the identification and apprehension of ringleaders and monetary backers of the pirate operation.

In a related resolution, the Security Council created an international committee to oversee more stringent control of all strategic arms production and deployment. The committee has been given the authority to decide on the disposition of the Israeli nuclear arms captured by the pirates during their lightning strikes. Informed sources surmise the plutonium from the weapons will be recycled into fuel rods and returned to Israel for use in civilian atomic power plants; the materials will then be monitored under the more watchful eye of the U.N.'s new international atomic energy agency.

B radley walked from his hotel along the wharf, letting the environment release his mind from thoughts too long dwelt upon. He looked slowly down long counters of iced-down crab and fish without stopping to buy. He watched tourists in camera carrying bliss as they in turn watched street musicians tuned to the beat of the dollar. He passed the Cannery without entering to browse the shops, continuing on to the bottom of the trolley car line. He regretted using the trolley almost as soon as he got on board, his sour mood only poisoned the many happier memories of prior trips up the hill. His walk down from the trolley stop to Chinatown was quick and effortless; in his reclusive thoughts, he nearly walked passed his street. Another half a block and he was at the Golden Dragon Restaurant.

Sharon was waiting at a small booth in the lounge. Their eyes met across the room. Bradley felt he was going to break into a run, grab her into his arms and kiss and cry; he resisted the surge of emotion, but increased his walking speed slightly. He felt more in control as he finished the remainder of the short walk. Her hair was pulled into a sophisticated knot, her beautiful features accentuated by meticulous makeup and by the lack of a distracting hair style. She wore a single pearl that fell near to where her deeply tanned skin met the décolletage of a thin, white dress with long sleeves.

"Hello, Share. You look very beautiful tonight."

"Thank you for coming, Mickey."

"I'm glad I came, you're a very nice dinner partner, you know. Would you like to order a drink?" He motioned to the bartender who came around the counter to take their order.

"Bushmills on the rocks and do you still like margaritas, Share?"

"That would be nice, Mickey."

"Margarita on the rocks and Bushmills on the rocks." The Chinese bartender placed small bar napkins with a yellow dragon print in front of them, then went back behind the bar to prepare the drinks.

"Mickey? About the other night."

"It's over Share, don't think about it."

"But, it was all my fault. I'm sorry."

"No, it wasn't your fault . . . it's not our fault. It's over . . . I don't want to talk about it now."

"Oh, Mickey. If only we could have waited a little."

"Look, Sharon, if you can't just let it go . . ."

The bartender brought their drinks. Bradley downed his in two big gulps, then passed the glass of ice back to the man, motioning for another before Sharon had tasted her first.

"Mickey? Will you tell me what's happened, or happening, to you? Whatever is wrong, I'm sure we, together, can cope with it."

"No, I don't believe we can handle it. It's too obscure. There is no place to get started. I've already made my moves and I don't know the game being played, but it's over now. I know it's over." His second drink came and he sipped it.

"I'd like to help. I love you, Mickey." He looked into her black eyes and only soft love resided there, he wanted to tell her everything, to lean on her, to trust her.

"I think they are going to kill me. They will find out what I know and kill me for knowing it."

"Who, Mickey? Who wants to kill you?"

"I don't know. No one — everyone. They are everywhere." The tone of her eyes changed to understanding.

"Mickey, whatever the problem there are people, trained people, who can help. Tell me what you think is wrong."

"I was one of them but something happened, I found out something they don't know. If they learn of it, they'll kill me." Her eyes held a whisper of doubt that grew until they became shaded with glassy muteness.

You've been reading the papers, he needed to tell her, *about all the fighting in the Mideast? The pirates in the Mideast? I'm one of them, I'm one of the pirates!* But this, his first thought, was translated into words as, "We've got to go now Sharon before they find out."

For the first God damn time, he thought, *I've got more essential data than their damn computer.* She continued to look at him dully, as if listening to directions in a foreign language. "Don't you see? They're treating me great now, but it won't last." *As soon as they figure out how I blew that lab, they'll have me again.* A glimmer of comprehension showed in her eyes and he thought at last she understood; her hand came across the table and rested on his forearm.

"Who's after you Mickey?"

"After me?. . . No one yet." Sympathy was welling out of her eyes. Bradley felt it gushing messily over the table. *It's hopeless*, he thought, *now she thinks I'm a paranoid.*

"God damn them! Samuel knew this was going to happen."

He stood up infuriated, partly at Sharon for acting the way she was and partly at Samuel for knowing she would beforehand.

"They know you now too . . . and there is nothing either of us can do about it." He bent over and kissed her lips lightly. He could feel the tears on her cheeks. "Good-bye, Sharon . . ."

Then a sickly humorous thought came to his mind and he smiled. He could see by Sharon's eyes that she thought it had all been some inappropriate joke. She seemed to be waiting for him to tell her so.

"Maybe our punch cards will come out together again sometime." He bent down and kissed her again, even more gently than before, dropped a bill on the table, then turned and walked away.

Bradley bought a bottle from a package store on his way back to his hotel on the wharf. He drank to deaden his feelings, to obscure his memories, but he could not sleep. Finally, he got into his old, yet somehow unfamiliar car and began to drive southward with neither deadline nor destination, the activity of driving a tool used to stave off the thoughts of his recent past. He drove as a means to attain the necessary state of exhaustion, fatigue that would allow him to slip swiftly from full wakefulness into mercifully thoughtless sleep. Sleep without the painful annoyance of disjointed, uncontrolled memories thrusting themselves into his susceptible dozing mind.

The first blinding light of morning glared through the window on which he had rested his head after falling asleep. He had parked the car in one of the many turn outs off California Highway 1, the narrow road that runs down the coast of California. He was alone on the top of a short bluff except for a group of seagulls that rambled awkwardly around the car. After attacking his bleary eyes with the flat part of his open hands, he groped for a cigarette. There were several open packages on the cluttered dashboard, but all of them were empty. He got out of the car, pulled off his jacket, tie, shirt, shoes, and socks, tossing them into a rumpled heap on the seat. He started to roll up the legs of his pants but his white legs contrasted sickly with the brown of his often exposed upper body, so he cut them off instead, starting with a knife cut and finishing with a tear.

Bradley was laying on his back in the sand, just beyond the surf, with one arm over his face, the crook of his elbow shielding his eyes from the sun, when he realized he was no longer alone. The man had come very close before Bradley heard his steps in the sand. He didn't bother to remove his arm as he really didn't care to see who it was.

"You're burning, Michael," the voice belonged to Samuel. "You missed the debriefing, I'm afraid." He was trying to get Bradley to look up at him and begin a conversation. If there was anyone Bradley didn't want to talk to, it was Samuel. "You're very hard on your clothing Michael . . . but no matter, I've brought a valise of things for you. Can't have you looking like a beachcomer in the city . . ." He knew how to goad him all right, but Bradley was determined to ignore him. "Beilikov has killed himself," he said quietly, finally getting through to Bradley. He pulled his arm away from his face and sat up facing the waves. Samuel continued to stand behind him.

"I bet you were just as surprised as you could be, too."

"As a matter of fact, Michael, the news did come as a shock. Beilikov had a very powerful instinct for survival."

Bradley turned and stood in one movement. Samuel stumbled backward as he had been standing even closer than Bradley thought – practically hovering over him.

"So he beat you at your own game, didn't he? He won the last hand, even if he did come out a big loser." Bradley was pleased that the Russian had surprised them, but devastated by the cost.

"His death was meaningless Michael . . . a terrible thing." He seemed genuinely grieved.

"Why? Did you have some future plans for him, Samuel? Is that it? Do you have to go to all the trouble of finding another to assume his role? Pardon me if I can't sympathize with your problem. I just can't help thinking, 'good for him, he out foxed the damn computer.' Speaking of which, I bet some programmer's got his ass in a sling over that one."

"No, Michael. His task was over. He had only to wait out the legal proceedings. We still don't understand what made him do it."

"Why, you jerk! Do you think he was so ignorant as to believe Bloc intelligence didn't know beforehand what was just around the corner from the Russian paratroop drop? He sent the air strike because by that time there was nothing else he could do. But he wasn't stupid enough to think you hadn't planned it that way from the start." Bradley was growing angrier with each word, for Beilikov's dilemma was also his own. He had found a solution and Bradley was still searching for his. "They planned to put him in a spot where he couldn't do anything but fry his own men!"

Bradley tried to summon up some appropriate slur to unleash on him, but none seemed vile enough. "You're low, Samuel — the lowest!"

"There was no other choice, Michael. The entire operation was already swinging into implementation. We were already committed by the time information of the illogical Syrian troop dispositions arrived. There was no other choice."

"And the Richardsons? I suppose there wasn't any choice on that one either was there? Send me in and let me murder them — the only way to do it right?" A long pause followed with Samuel's sorrowful eyes staring into Bradley's.

"Yes, that's correct."

Bradley almost went for him, but he feared they expected him to do something like that and he didn't want to do anything they expected. He kicked sand up on Samuel's immaculate suit in ineffectual rage.

"Well, you can forget about me, too. As far as the Bloc is concerned, I'm also dead. No more missions, no more killing, no more dancing at the end of your strings."

"You're fortunate to be able to simply walk away from it all now. And don't delude yourself; we know that's just what you're going to do."

This was the only time Bradley had ever seen him angry. He didn't know if it was what he had said or just the sand he was trying uselessly to brush off his dark suit.

"Only there are thousands of others who were captured after we flew you out. Thousands that depend on us to coordinate their defense from our freedom. You have no more missions. Your job is finished, but we need to debrief you so we can wage an efficient legal defense. We have to know about the laboratory."

"No debriefing either," Bradley said flatly.

Samuel was surprised. His mouth dropped open and he stopped brushing his stomach with his handkerchief. Bradley was trying to think of some valid reason. He couldn't tell him the truth, that he was afraid to let them know how he had blown the laboratory. He had to say something to prevent the debriefing. He knew that they would find out in a detailed rendition of what had happened no matter how hard he tried to lie around the catalytic reaction. He decided to toss Samuel a bone.

"I got there and everyone was dead but the Richardsons. They had infected them with something; I don't know what . . . They gave me a shot so I wouldn't get it. I wired the armory up and split out to the rim of the valley. When it blew, I started walking. That's it. That's all I know. That's the debriefing." Bradley started walking back up the beach toward the little bluff where three cars were parked — his old greed Ford, a long, black limo and a sleek, silver Porsche.

Samuel made it up the small sand cliff without falling too far behind. At the cars, Bradley noticed a dark suited man at the wheel of his Ford. When he turned to Samuel to complain, the old green car pulled out and clunked off northward.

"The new car is yours, Michael . . . no strings. As I've said, your task is finished. All the details have been taken care of: keys, registration, checkbook, credit cards, clothing. Everything is in the car. Take a vacation; try to forget. We all did terrible, unavoidable things, but now we need to learn to live with them." He was lightly serious, obviously enjoying the feeling of a father on Christmas morning.

"No debriefing?" Bradley searched his face for the telltale signs of deception, but found none.

"As you said on the beach, that was the debriefing. If that is all you will give, that is all we will have. We should be able to piece the rest together from other sources, but Michael, I can't promise that the trials will go well without you. If you decide to help us, call this number." He handed Bradley a card with a toll free number under his single name.

"I will do my best to keep you out of the remainder of this ordeal. You have done so much more than we expected already. Good-bye, Michael." He put out his hand in a gesture of let bygones be bygones. Bradley swallowed his pride and shook it.

"Good-bye, Samuel. I hope I don't upset you by saying I hope I never see you again."

"No, I quite understand your feelings." He got into the waiting car. Bradley was soon standing alone again, only this time beside a brand new car. He touched his thighs and realized Samuel had been right again. He had been burning. He looked in the car and on the passenger's seat were a pair of sandals and a white polo shirt with a tube of tanning oil in the breast pocket. "They think of everything."

When he pulled the sports car out onto the road, he was hoping that they hadn't been able to guess what he was considering. He was thinking about trying to run, to lose himself in the millions of people and thousands of miles that made up the United States, to bury himself so deeply that by the time they figured out how he had blown the lab they wouldn't be able to find him — find him and end the knowledge of catalytic fusion.

The car was nice, but if he chose to run, it would have to go, along with the rest of the stuff that would make him easy to find. He was playing with the problem of how to exchange the checking account balance and credit card limits into cash when he realized it would probably only delay the inevitable.

Robert Stone had given volumes of information to the Security Council's special piracy committee during the long sessions of open interrogation. He had explained his role in bringing the pirate Bloc's military units into their Mideast target areas under a United Nations disguise. He told them of grand motives and unselfish goals. He presented a long report on the genetics laboratory in Libya the pirate Bloc had destroyed. He quoted horrifying statistical estimates of probable casualties had the laboratory's findings been permitted to be used in a genetic war. He explained they had been forced into their unprecedented action by the need for rapid, yet totally secret, strikes to accomplish their altruistic mission.

He did not answer questions pertaining to the Bloc's ultimate leadership, nor those delving into the mystery of its funding. He also left huge gaps in his explanation of the Bloc's superior intelligence gathering capabilities. Stone restrained himself from telling all of what he knew; however, even he would have been amazed at how little that actually was.

While the hearings were not in session Stone was being held in a relaxed, if conspicuous, house arrest at his uptown New York City apartment. The United States, and especially the President, wanted it to be internationally apparent that Stone's actions were not of an official nature. Two agents of the Federal Bureau of Investigation stayed with him in his apartment; one always remaining awake. Another two alternated as backup eyes to the building's security guards as they watched closed circuit television monitors in the building's lobby. Everyone was quite sure that Stone would not suddenly disappear.

When John Yazzee checked through the lobby's security center with a signature and a call to the fourteenth floor apartment he was visiting, he was also sure Stone wouldn't leave the building unexpectedly. Yazzee was a huge young man with short black hair and deep soft brown eyes. His olive skin contrasted warmly against the crisp white shirt he wore beneath his well-tailored three-piece suit. He carried himself with the grace of a dancer of ballet and the latent strength of a football player. He was well mannered and manicured. He could have been an attorney or a broker on his way to visit a client or friend, but he wasn't. The old couple on the fourteenth floor who cleared his entrance had never met the insurance agent they expected to call on them that afternoon.

It would be true to say that Mr. Yazzee worked for no insurance company; yet he did in his own way deal in insurance. He went to the apartment on the fourteenth floor and obligatorily discussed a life insurance package with his first clients, leaving abundant literature for them to read before he made his leisurely exit. He then climbed the stairs to the seventeenth floor.

At Stone's door he produced identification that proved him to be yet another agent of the FBI. Once inside, the two genuine agents proved not to be a sufficient match for him. With his gun to the head of one them, he convinced both to disarm, then effortlessly clubbed them into unconsciousness with the hardened edge of his hand. When they awoke, they found him long gone and ex-United States Ambassador to the United Nations, Robert Stone, sitting back in his favorite recliner, his throat neatly cut.

The Porsche's momentary loss of traction on the metal rails of the street car line caused the wide low tires each to sound a staccato chirp as Bradley rounded Lee Circle. In the daytime, the ill-timed lights, racing multidirectional traffic, and recklessly massive street cars made the trip 'roundabout' the statue an especially handy place to be driving a sports car. The agility of the car made it easier to race into a transient gap in the circular saw spinning around the feet of General Lee. The expensive German sports car also served another valuable service: that of camouflage. It helped make the transition into Uptown New Orleans smoother, helping Bradley live without notice in the upscale Garden District of the grand old city. But the night was fading and traffic was light even for the late hour.

The beauty of the trip uptown passed quickly before his now more tired than intoxicated eyes. The canopy of Louisiana oak over park like St. Charles Avenue produced an indoor effect and the architecture of the historic old mansions gleamed magically in the illusion. He swung the car across the woodsy divider and dodged a street car to u-turn into the opposing traffic lane. After backtracking a half block, he turned up the cobblestone drive of the fairytale stone house, parking in front of the wrought iron gate that opened into the carport side of the courtyard.

Bradley had only been in New Orleans ten days when the key to the house had been sent to him at the Royal Sonesta Hotel. Upon driving uptown to the address on the key chain, he had found the house complete from the clothes in the closet to the drain board in the kitchen. A slip of paper that had been taped to the thoughtfully stocked refrigerator read, "Enjoy! Samuel." And for two weeks he had been giving it a good try.

He walked up the flagstone path from the pedestrian gate, surrounded by a healthy lawn kept manicured by a gardener he had never seen. Under the bright light of the front door vestibule he fumbled with his key a moment before he could get the door to unlock. He hit the light switch as he crossed into the room, but it remained dark. He stood silhouetted against the bright light of the doorway, waiting for his eyes to adjust before crossing the dark room to another light switch.

"Bang." The voice was flat from lack of emotion. Bradley's mind pulled up a memory of another time, another door way, and he recognized the voice as the old man in the desert a lifetime before.

"You're a damn fool boy!" His voice was slow and brittle, seemingly without origin in the blackness to which Bradley's eyes were fighting to adjust. If he only knew where he was, he might be able to jump out of the light and go for him in the darkness.

"I knew they would send someone for me, but I hadn't expected it to be you."

"Maybe you're not such a fool after all. You say you've been expecting a visit?" Bradley had the location of his voice narrowed to one corner of the room and his eyes were beginning to see objects. If he had any chance, this was it. He threw himself to one side of the shaft of light coming through the doorway and rolled into a four point crouch. His eyes ached from the ineffectual widening of his lids. Then he heard his old trainer laugh the friendly way he used to when Bradley had done something well during his training, but not quite perfectly.

"That's real good, boy. Your eyes adjusted already?" With another laugh, the interior lights switched on, blinding him again. The game was over; the old guy had won. Bradley stood up still blinking.

"So Samuel thought I was important enough to send you here personally?" Bradley's eyes were beginning to return to normal.

"Samuel's dead, boy. Didn't you know?" He was sitting back in a leather recliner. His feet were off the floor and his hands were clasped on his abdomen. Not the position to kill someone from. He was in a dark three-piece suit with a narrow black tie and a white shirt. His hair was short, but dark around the edges of his head. His bald pate gave him the air of a jolly, if ineffectual salesman. He saw Bradley looking him over and smiled.

"This isn't Death Valley, boy, a man must dress for his terrain . . . and his enemy."

"Who killed him?"

"At first I thought it was you." His sun bleached eyes still held the wary challenge of the street fighter Bradley had grown accustomed to in the desert. "But it was too messy. Not the kind of killing you do at all."

"I don't kill now. I'm out of it."

"Don't get upset, boy. I'm not saying that you enjoyed it or that it could have been avoided. It's just that on occasion you have killed. How can I say it? And on those occasions it has been . . . neatly from a distance."

Bradley's mind recovered the suppressed memory of an incident in Vietnam . . . The Lieutenant was looking through the glasses out over the edge of the hill where the two-man sniper team was stationed. Bradley and his teammate lay on either side of the weapon. Bradley had his right arm around it and his right eye to the scope. He could see the target clearly. A North Vietnamese fuel truck was broken down. The bed was piled precariously high with gas cans and two North Vietnamese regulars with AK-47s stood guard.

"Yep. That would be quite a shot." The Lieutenant turned to them and handed Bradley the four red-tipped cartridges. "I still think it's too far."

"Bottle a hooch, Loot?" Dave goaded him, jumping at the chance to make a bet.

"Hey we only got four rounds of this stuff, Dave." Bradley was also pretty sure the distance was too great.

"That's all right, Mike, one to get range and one to score." Bradley shrugged. If they missed, the two of them would split the cost of the booze. Bradley nodded he was in.

"All right, you guys are on," the Lieutenant laughed.

Bradley loaded one of the tracer rounds into the weapon, then brought it back up to his shoulder. He placed the crosshair on the truck, raised it over the top, over the trees behind, and finally onto a gray sky with darker gray clouds. He squeezed off the shot and had plenty of time to bring the crosshair back down to the target. Short.

"I told you guys it was too far," the Lieutenant said. The shot had fallen in the rice paddy just in front of the crude road where the truck was stalled. Bradley no longer felt it was an impossible distance.

"I don't know, Lieutenant, we still got a little leeway." He handed the weapon to Dave. "I aimed about another tree height up in the air."

"OK partner, I'm going about a half one above that." Bradley heard the concussion and watched through his field glasses as he waited for the artillery like round to cover the distance. The guards jerked to readiness when they heard the sound of the hit.

"Nice shot, Dave. That means we win, right?" Bradley looked up to the Lieutenant.

"No way, Bradley. You got to finish the job."

"Full cans just don't go up like empty ones," Dave said regretfully, still sighting with the scope. The guards were looking all around in the nearby jungle and examining the ground underneath the truck.

"Looks like some of those cans won't be full for long."

"All right, your shot Bradley." The Lieutenant wanted him to shoot while the cans were still full. He loaded the weapon slowly and took his time as he aimed for the spot one and a half tree lengths over the top of the jungle. He fired, but couldn't regain the target with the scope before the round hit.

"All right, partner, you poked some more holes in 'er," Dave spoke as he tried to regain the target. Then he could see the truck again; the guards were running around it terrified. They knew what was happening now but they were helpless; to leave the truck would get them killed by their buddies, to stay by it would risk a bullet. They solved the problem by taking cover under the front of the truck.

"OK. One more, then you guys loose. Hurry up, take the shot."

Bradley was watching through the glasses when he heard the blast of Dave's shot. He could see the white streak of the tracer against the darkening sky just before it reached the target. A huge billow of white orange flame burst into the grayness and Dave let out a joyous hoot. Bradley watched as one of the guards, burning from head to foot, stumbled toward the rice paddy in front of the blazing truck; he fell, short of the paddy, and burned in the middle of the road.

"All right, I owe you two killers a bottle." The Lieutenant handed back the glasses and started to go. "And make sure you clean than phosphorous out of your weapon." Bradley blinked the memory away and his thoughts returned to New Orleans.

"You know what I mean, boy . . . you got a certain technique, and breaking into Samuel's house and cutting his throat while he was asleep isn't your style."

"No, I guess not. Who, then?"

"Who? Well, could be that boy I trained after you – a big Indian kid from Arizona. Six and a half feet of clean cut, well educated, fine mannered heee-roo." The innocuous salesman flashed eyes of contempt. "Took everything a lot more seriously than you; much more willing to learn. He ran and lifted weights in his spare time. Quick as a jackrabbit. Matter of fact, he could run one down in a couple hours, never saw anything like it – he'd just take off after one and keep after it until the damn thing gave up. Bring them back by the ears; still alive, but in some kind of shock. Sit them in the corner where they sat perfectly still until they finally toppled over dead."

"So he had the same desert training I did."

"Well, we kind of called that part off . . . he didn't much need it, you see."

"What about the rest?"

"Took him up to Chicago for awhile and trained in the city."

"Who does he work for?"

"Last I heard . . . Samuel."

"But, you think he killed Samuel?"

"I don't really know . . . I feel only two people alive could have completed that mission . . . you would have did it a little differently. Not so messy, you know."

"How can we find him?"

The old man smiled the sly smile he seemed to hold when he possessed knowledge he was about to transfer to an apprentice.

"He'll find you, boy . . . as a matter of fact, I was a little surprised to find you were still alive."

"I'll stay alive." Bradley's mind flashed to the Richardsons passive acceptance of death and realized he would never yield his life, even for the life of a loved one. "I could use a little help working in the cities."

"Yeah, I know. But there isn't time. We meet Barkman in the morning for breakfast."

"Joe Barkman? What does he have to do with all of this?"

"Well, he seems to think he has this all figured out . . . he has been working with the computer you know. He sent me a letter that convinced me to come down here."

"Does Barkman know who we're working for?"

"Are we working for someone?"

"We have so far."

"You're right . . . but I don't think we're working for anyone now. We have too many pieces of the puzzle to work with."

"Where will we meet?"

"Brennan's at eleven o'clock. Ramos Fizzes and eggs Benedict." The old man stood up and smoothed down accumulated wrinkles from his suit.

"See you in the morning at Brennan's," the old man said over his shoulder as he walked toward the gate. Bradley stood in the doorway watching him go, then he called after him.

"Hey I don't even know your name."

The cagey old soldier laughed aloud as he answered, "Harold Wilson of Wilson Electronics . . . automatic garage door openers, you know." With this, the old man disappeared into the damp, predawn blackness.

Joe Barkman had always been adversely impressed by needless pretentions and had expressed his scorn of the academic charade lived by many of his peers by his uniquely casual, yet unadulterated dress. He had found satisfaction, while attending the myriad social obligations of a tenured Professor, in always being properly attired yet not overly so.

But on this gray, drizzling morning in New Orleans he selected his gray tweed suit, a thin black tie, and a crisp white shirt from the negligible wardrobe he had brought with him from California. He hung them neatly on the bathroom doorknob, the thin blue cellophane from the drycleaners dragging the floor. He shaved first, as was his custom, then took a cool shower which was also his custom in the morning. He would wait until just prior to dressing to brush his hair and teeth. After drying, he put on a terrycloth robe and dialed room service for coffee and a croissant. He had deliberately requested an early wakeup call so he could review his papers one last time before meeting for brunch the two men he needed desperately to convince of his sanity. He wanted to be sure of all his facts so he would be prepared for their inevitable questions.

He sat at the austere writing desk that had a clothes bureau at the other end. The tall table lamp cast a dull light down on his briefcase as he removed the four-inch pile of paper. The dimness caused his eyes to strain as he read over portions of the photocopies that hadn't been clearly reproduced. He silently damned the pseudo convenience offered by hotels in general and the true annoyances of this one in particular as he unconsciously reached for a cup of coffee that hadn't yet arrived. He crossed the room to the phone and dialed room service again — no answer. He redialed to receive a busy signal. On the third try, he let the phone ring endlessly.

"Room Service."

"Yes. I'm in Room 206. I called for coffee and a croissant forty minutes ago. Is this normal, or has there been some mix up?"

"Well, sir. I really don't know, let me check." The familiar silence of being on hold filled his ear. He cursed aloud, but to his surprise the room service operator came back on the line almost immediately.

"Sir? The order was just sent up. I'm sorry about the wait."

"All right. Thank you."

He was replacing the receiver when the knock came on the door. A muffled voice carried into the room, "Room Service."

B radley saw the old man from across the room as he was led to the table at Brennan's. He held a Times Picayune out to one side of the table with his right hand and a large creamy white drink with his left. A small cherry wood pipe hung unlit from his mouth, the role of salesman being played to perfection. He read intently until Bradley was being seated, then with a rustle of paper he turned back to the table. The pipe disappeared and the drink was affectionately placed by his setting. He stood slightly as he shook Bradley's hand vigorously.

"How are you, Bradley? Have a drink, this place makes the best Ramos Fizz in the world." He motioned to the waiter with the first two fingers of his thick hand. A hand that seemed a little too callused and hard for a salesman.

Bradley sat opposite the apparently ineffectual Midwestern roadman who had been reading from a large assortment of the area's major newspapers. The man who had taught Bradley so much about the desert noticed him surveying the voluminous collection.

"The media is attempting to make Stone into a martyr or a hero, it seems. Evidently they don't care about the loss of any information he held."

"They control the media." Bradley's drink arrived and he tasted it with a sneer. "These aren't bad if you hold your nose, they stink like toilet water."

"That's true about the Bloc's influence over the news media, of course. Which brings me to another item they seem to be paying special attention to — the boy who calls himself Brother. Have you been keeping up with his escapades?"

"I heard he claims to be able to cure the sick."

"The claims are made by the media or people of his entourage; he has yet to make any statement."

"What is this anyway? Are we going to talk current events that have no meaning for us or are we going to meet Barkman?"

"No, Mike, we're not. The subject Barkman wanted to discuss with us concerned the boy's connection with our own problems. As it is, he will never be able to present his own evidence. I went by his hotel this morning to give him a lift. The police were just having his body removed."

"I need a drink. Not this smelly shit, but a real drink!"

Bradley again found himself on an airplane over the Atlantic Ocean. Only this trip was as frilled as his first had been austere. He reclined in the thickly cushioned, first class seat of a wide bodied luxury airliner. An untouched drink filled a recess in the hardwood cocktail tray between himself and his reticent companion. Attractively young, brightly uniformed flight attendants with arms full of head phones and magazines, and faces wide with white on pink smiles, seemed to appear spontaneously if he so much as twisted to a more comfortable position.

Yet Bradley's state of mind was unaffected by any of the physical comforts. He was as apprehensive as he had been on the long C-5A flight to his first mission at the laboratory in Libya. His unfocused eyes gazed out into the darkness of the flight-shortened night, the wild claims Barkman had made before his death clouding his mind. Before the abortive rendezvous in New Orleans, Barkman had mailed a thick packet of pirated documents to the apparently ineffectual salesman, Wilson. His revelations still seemed to Bradley almost too spectacular for reality.

The idea that an entity existed that was only partially human and that this entity was manipulating major world events and the lives of uncounted millions of people filled Bradley with disgust of the ease of his own manipulation. He couldn't rationalize away his feeling of having been used casually by a near human to cause the end of human life. He wasn't confident that Wilson's choice of action was viable or even appropriate, but he needed to strike back. Desperately wanting to contravene the computer's prediction of the future, he had agreed to accompany Wilson on what he felt was a somewhat Quixotesque mission of assassination.

He attempted to make himself believe that Wilson was correct in his opinion that they could be sufficiently unpredictable to succeed, but his mind continued to retrieve incidents from the recent past where he had inadvertently performed as life's prior conditioning induced him. He turned to Wilson to speak, but found him no longer in the seat opposite his own. He turned to look down the aisle and a plastic smile shined down on him.

"Mr. Wilson has gone to the lounge. Can I show you the way, sir?"

"No, thank you, I'm fine here." Bradley dimmed his reading lamp then leaned back to try to sleep. The flight attendant instantly produced a pillow.

Bradley and his onetime trainer had agreed that the plan best suited to their particular capabilities and deficiencies would be an ambush of the unprotected youth known as "Brother." That being their best chance of success, it was their next logical action. But they knew that action would be expected, so they had decided to instead break the power of the man-machine gestalt at its computer component rather than the human.

They realized that they had only a miniscule chance of ever getting close enough to the computer to do it physical harm, but they had learned that holographic computer systems were very susceptible to power fluctuations. They also knew, however, that the E.E.C. primary holographic computer in Brussels had more than adequate independent back-up generating capacity. Enough capacity to keep its power input at a constant and precise level in the case of a blackout of the more general grid system.

The back-up generating units almost never ran. Occasionally they would be started and a full diagnostic test array would be investigated, but they had never been required to supply energy to their only conceivable service load. The four huge, stoically silent combustion turbines awaited a signal to instantly start and immediately send energy along private lines the short distance to the E.E.C. central computer. Ninety inch headers pulled cooling water from the Scheldt to be used as the blood of its steel vascular system. Clarifiers and multi-train demineralizers purified some of the water to the purest levels for pre-turbine injection. Voluminous fuel tanks, filled languidly from underground pipelines, could keep the turbines running for a month. And while five human maintenance men spent their time servicing instruments and automatic controls, the E.E.C. holographic computer controlled all operations remotely.

Their plan depended on the hope that the protective circuits guarding against sudden power spikes might be inadequate beyond the level of conventionally produced power surges. If they could bring the input power to the computer protective systems to some vaguely defined high range, the protection system might fail from overload. And if the protection circuits failed, high input energy to the laser generated holographic system would cause an uncontrolled increase in the laser's light intensity, forcing irreparable damage to delicate holographic information storage components.

They knew these things because the Bloc computer had supplied the information. The packet sent by Barkman before his death contained the elaborate procedure he had developed for the undetected extraction of restricted data from the Bloc systems computer. But even as they used the procedure, they knew that Barkman had probably not gone as undetected as he had believed.

A young college student and several aging World War II veterans manned the box like security hut at the front gate. The security hut was overcrowded with kitchen appliances and soft chairs to make it more comfortable for the guards to eat and sometimes sleep. The college student had never shot a gun at another human being and the old WW II vets didn't want to think about it. They all liked driving the new truck around the station perimeter. They would drink chocolate spiked with espresso from the mouths of thermos bottles and smoke mild European cigarettes, so satisfyingly full of nicotine and tar, while the totally domesticated German Shepherd guard dogs would run alongside the truck until they got tired and jumped up into the bed.

The night was clear and razor cold. Batieste, the Botany major at the University of Gent, was bored. His two companions were busily cutting fresh vegetables to eat with their meal of baked flounder. And when the nightly argument over the spices to be added to the food brought color to both of their portly faces, Batieste offered to make the rounds in the truck.

The two large puppy-mannered shepherds jumped into the bed and scratched on the rear window of the cab, much too spoiled to endure the icy night air without a minor protest. Once the truck began to move, their objections faded under the brilliance of sounds and scents common to the area at night. They ran continuously around the small truck bed until their frost activated energy thrust them out and down to the hard cold ground. They ran ahead so they could stop to identify pheromone markings then make their mark in turn before running to overtake the truck.

Batieste nibbled on bread and cheese as he followed the high fence around the generating station, making sure all was as it should be. He released the steering wheel to unscrew the cap of his thermos and as he pressed his knee to the wheel, the truck slowed and the dogs streaked by on either side. Something about their continual barking had changed. No longer were they sounding like the overgrown puppies he had always known them to be. They suddenly sounded vicious, even ferocious. He rescrewed the cap, placed the bottle alongside his dry meal on the seat, then taking the wheel in both hands, accelerated in the truculent wake of the dogs.

He found them running and leaping against the thick chain link of the fence. He stopped the truck adjacent to where they centered their grim attention. The fence was cut. Tiny insulated loops of wire held the breach closed. Long color coded jumper wires with alligator clipped ends retained the electrical continuity that if interrupted caused alarms to sound in the guard's tiny kitchen and a signal to be sent to the central computer.

With the dogs still barking wildly, eyes and teeth shining in the glare of the headlights, he reached out his hand to remove one of the startling wires. The barking ceased without a whimper and the dogs lay dead at his feet. He pulled back his hand when a voice in impeccable French commanded him not to move. Two darkly dressed men approached from the other side of the fence, armed with large pistols fitted with silencing devices.

"Back away from the fence with your hands away from your body." Batieste extended his arms in a child-like parody of an airplane, then took long slow steps backward. "That's far enough." One of the men stooped, cut the temporary wire stitches from the opening then passed lithely through. He pushed Batieste chest first against the truck and by pulling on various limbs moved him to the classic stance of one to be searched. As it was being done, the other man, the man who had spoken, came through the fence.

"We don't want to hurt you, but we will if we must." He was placed in the bed of the truck, shackled hand and foot, gagged and blinded with a thick woolen hood. He was shaking with fear and cold as the truck bumped toward the center of the power plant.

Not far away small muffled explosions severed a dozen high voltage lines that supplied power to the city of Brussels. The four combustion turbines immediately came to life and within minutes were supplying power directly to the mammoth complex housing the European Economic Community's central holographic computer.

Bradley and Wilson drove directly to the computer control room where five instrument technicians watched the machines race to their required load. The technicians had long prepared for this moment and yet they were unprepared for it. The long months of nonoperation had conditioned them to the quietly inactive systems; it was a surprise to them when voluminous forced draft fans began to scream and combustion turbines started to roar. They had all gravitated separately to the automated control room, still in a somewhat dazed state. Now they watched as digital printouts from all their carefully calibrated instruments glowed simultaneously for the first time. As the automated analyses data came in, chemical pumps responded with corresponding green lights, valves opened or closed causing more blinking, fuel addition rates varied with red numbers changing rapidly, the entire plant was a vividly living entity. They were engrossed by the sudden change in their mundane routine and the enormity of the machines operating beyond the control of any human.

Any human except one who was so much more, who at this moment silently pondered the meaning of the simultaneous loss of all his power supply except the private power plant he had never believed he would need to use. The repair crews were sent out and the backup systems had functioned as planned, but the failure was unmistakably deliberate. He analyzed the data intensely even though he was a thousand kilometers away. In moments he came to the conclusion that the men with guns he had expected to meet in this self were at this time attacking his other self, far away.

Was this one feeble attempt at cutting his power the entire plan, or was it only a diversion for another more dangerous action? He knew they were in Europe, but they had quickly disappeared shortly after their arrival. They could be in Brussels, fleeing from failure or pursuing their attack, or they could be just outside his own door. He realized they were desperately trying not to react as they should by past stimulus-response conditioning. They had succeeded so far, but the open attack? Did Bradley still believe his victory in Libya was his own?

Brother lay down on the sagging metal bed in the youth hostel, but didn't sleep. He knew that if the last power supply to the part of himself made of light and metal and plastic and mineral crystal hardware was discontinued he would no longer be complete. If the power plant was shut down, the final, battery backup system had only one hour of energy storage capacity. If the repair crews couldn't restore power in less than an hour of that last severing, a part of himself wouldn't exist until the intricate patterns of laser light were resupplied with energy. He didn't know what it would be like to be less than himself and it frightened him. He knew it would be a maddening but hopefully temporary retardation. He closed his eyes to prepare himself for any of the possible eventualities. The trance-like state could easily have been mistaken for sleep, but he remained alert while he waited.

When Wilson and Bradley secured the control room, they found the instrument technicians strangely docile and cooperative. They appeared to be in mild shock. Bradley stood guard as Wilson questioned them in his surprising French. The instrument techs showed them where the load indicators were located and also showed them how they could be decalibrated to indicate spuriously low values. Once done the computer saw 100 megawatts as 50 megawatts.

Bradley smiled thinly when the load began to increase, amazed that the only other load control was on the normal, external energy supply circuit. The load increased to maximum and the load indicators were decalibrated another twenty-five percent, then again by twelve and a half, then six and a fourth.

Within the holographic computer laser light intensities grew and processor temperatures rose. Plastic and insulation melted, monochromatic crystals cracked, and structural metals expanded and snapped. Less than a minute at the elevated power levels and the powerful holographic computer was a smoldering ruin. At that moment a young, well educated American Indian named Yazzee heard the voice he believed to be God. He began packing his bag after booking a flight reservation for Belgium.

As Bradley and Wilson left the control room, with its bound and gagged technicians, Brother fell into a sweaty, cold skinned, high temperature, muscle twitching coma. His small entourage began a twenty four hour prayer vigil at his bedside. Brother silently, yet immediately, ordered the delivery of a new virginal holographic computer. He couldn't expect any help carrying the entire European computer load until a new hardware system was delivered. Yet, with an almost imperceptible blink, the computerized information systems of Europe continued almost as normal.

Brother had never endured such unmitigated pain. His body felt like a child's balloon frantically deflating, spilling wildly its unthrottled jet of inner contents. The large muscles of his body and his internal organs were being dismembered molecule by molecule for their energy content. His breath changed rapidly from its normal scent to the smelly stench of acetone. His followers mercifully nursed his scalding body with ice packs without effect. They repeatedly changed his bedding, so quickly fouled with perspiration and the pitiful products of uncontrolled, yet empty bowels. They spooned water and soup into his mouth but he remained immobile. Finally, they called for a doctor to administer to the earthly flesh of the being they loudly proclaimed to be the Savior.

As the doctor tried frantically to replace Brother's blood electrolytes intravenously, the media seized upon the human interest of the event. They republished accounts of the march of healing across Europe. They interviewed his small, but growing, group of worshippers whenever and wherever they were found. The media provided the vehicle for these followers to bring one of their most adamant claims into almost every country of the world. Over and over again the televisions showed a near hysterical believer blaming the holographic computer's "Sickness" for the loss of their God. For by this time it was common knowledge that Brother had been stricken at as close to the same instant as the computer's destruction as could be determined. The question on every Europeans' lips was the pointed, "how can it still work?" How could the entire socioeconomic labyrinth of computer dependent Europe still be functioning without the most complicated computer system in the world?

The worshippers of Brother claimed he was curing the computer system with his own life's energy. The Government simply stated another computer was at that moment being preprogrammed. The Governmental announcements failed to state that Brother, an adolescent boy far away across the continent, was personally bringing the new computer hardware into the thinking world.

In Rome, a small story on a back page of a daily newspaper announced the suicide of a quiet old veterinarian. The story didn't receive any air time on television.

W ilson bled. His left forearm was mangled from the unmer-
cifully soft metal of the bullet. He squeezed his handkerchief to the cavernous hole with his taut right hand as he
ran down the narrow dark street. He had been ambushed and it
made his anger burn in the back of his throat. How long had he
worked at his so comfortably safe way of life? So many sacrifices made
to be ready for a moment like this and he had fallen head first into
a ridiculously obvious trap. He knew now that the heady success at
the power plant had shaded his judgment. He had only lost a few
moments of reaction time, but it had meant the difference between a
quick victory and running wounded from a relentless pursuer.

He had seen the Indian in plenty of time, but he had made the
mistake of believing Yazzee would talk. Instead, his former student
had answered his cautious salutation with the muffled voice of a
silenced handgun. Wilson knew that if the wall he had leapt with
bullets flying around him had been only slightly higher, he would
already be dead. As things stood now, as he ran with one arm holding the other together, he knew it was only a matter of time before
his large, young adversary overtook his rhythmless, stumbling pace.
He remembered the Indian's clockwork strides from Death Valley.

He had watched Yazzee pace himself behind a jackrabbit until the rabbit had run itself to death. He decided he would rather face the moment with as much strength as possible. He found a good spot and stopped running.

The young Indian had predetermined that the trainer would die without the chance to fight, he had carefully placed himself in a position of ambush that gave him long moments to fire his weapon unopposed. But Yazzee was not a man of ambush; he was not as adept with silenced handguns as he was with razors. This catharsis from a stealthy hunter to the distasteful role of bushwhacker had been motivated from fear.

The young man, Yazzee, had changed his technique because of a subliminal fear of Wilson's talent for survival. As he followed his wounded prey, this became clear to him in a violent wave of self disgust. He realized that had he used his more accustomed procedure in all probability he wouldn't be tracking a wounded, forewarned, well-trained man through the wet back streets of Brussels. He no longer cared if Wilson was armed, he put his pistol at the bottom of a trash can as he passed and retrieved the razor from his jacket pocket.

As Yazzee jogged down the wet alley, he passed very close to his prey, now hidden in a shadow darkened alcove. He continued to the more amply illuminated corner where his relentless pace slowed, then stopped. He knew this situation well; the prey had abandoned its flight in favor of concealment. He knew Wilson was nearby, waiting to see if he would safely pass, hiding in the darkness, watching him standing in the light. He turned toward the dark alley. His quiet voice carried vibrantly over the wet stones.

"Come and die in the light, Wilson, or you will die in the darkness."

"What difference does it make, boy?" Wilson stepped into the small vaguely defined circle of light the Indian occupied on the corner. Yazzee smiled in approval as he took inventory of his prior trainer now beginning to show his years. He was shirtless, his broad shoulders square and hard in appearance. His left arm was tied in a viciously tight shoe string tourniquet just above his elbow. His feet were bare and solidly placed on the slippery stone. His right arm hung loosely to his side, the familiar bayonet in his hand pointing to the pavement. Yazzee pulled off his leather soled shoes then his silk stockings, then his jacket, tie and shirt.

"You're hurt, Wilson. My bullet made you a cripple."

"Only in body, son, only in body."

There should not have been any contest between the two seemingly mismatched opponents. The one so young and strong and tireless, the other growing older and weaker and more tired with each drop of blood lost to the ancient paving stones of the dirty gutter. They knew each other very well in the discipline of knife fighting. The outcome was neither swift nor one-sided. Yet in the end it was as both knew it would be — an exhausted young man with multiple bayonet wounds walked alone from the late night encounter.

B radley read a newspaper he had bought at a newsstand on the way to the airport, his under graduate German more than adequate to surmise the meaning of the stories. When he came to the story of the unidentified man who had been murdered and mutilated in the back streets of Brussels, he shuddered. He had gone to the morgue to see the body for himself; it had definitely been his old trainer from Death Valley. He had stared at his friend until the demands of the authorities required him to identify the body or leave. He left. The memory of the dead man with a score of razor cuts on his upper body and the shattered left forearm and the head neatly severed from the neck, floated in front of the unfamiliar language on the page. He knew that the Indian was looking for him. He knew it would probably come to a kill or be killed situation. He hoped he could avoid such an encounter because he knew any man who could find and destroy Wilson would probably be capable of doing the same to him. He refolded the paper and turned off the narrow beam reading lamp that glared down from the overhead console. He closed his eyes, trying to sleep on yet another airplane. This time it was an El Al commuter flight from Rome to Jerusalem.

He had arrived in Rome to find the city a flurry of conjecture and prayer. The city was buzzing with excitement following the healing in the streets of dozens of physically handicapped pilgrims by an adolescent boy who called himself Brother. The boy had left Rome, stating publically only that his people needed him in Jerusalem. Bradley had doubts that a boy that cured the sick with his touch could have ordered the decapitation of his friend, Wilson; but he had boarded the plane for Israel with them in check. He was alone now and he mustn't let his doubts make him an easy target. He mustn't let the most detailed knowledge of the one called Brother disappear at the end of a knife. He had to survive. He had to find the boy and if he was truly the one behind a bloody war, uncounted murders, and the indirect control of the actions of so many helpless human beings, he would kill him.

As he had been unable to sleep on so many other planes, so it was on this one. He switched the light back on and returned to his struggle with the German language newspaper. The settlement in the Middle East was the predominant news, as it had been for the past week, since the news of the newly commissioned E.E.C. holographic computer had grown stale. In shocking, simultaneous announcements, Israel and the Moslem Bloc had proclaimed the creation of a Palestinian state on the west bank of the Jordan River.

Worldwide pressure and the realization of hopeless political positions had forced the two sides not to agree, but to agree not to disagree. The cornerstone of the plan was the creation of an international city of Jerusalem, with the war devastated Mount of Olives, Dome of the Rock area made into a park-like garden with no structures permitted. All religious viewpoints would have equal access to the holy spot, yet none could build permanent materialistic tributes. The temples would have no more physical substance than the beliefs they represented. Moslem, Hebrew, and Christian services would be held in the open air of the finely manicured gardens. The Mosque of Omar was to be rebuilt from the ancient rubble at one edge of the reserve. A magnificent Christian cathedral was to be erected on another edge and the Temple of Solomon was to go on yet another. The holy site they surrounded would be open to all.

Bradley shuddered when he again read of the preparations the Jews were making for their first service on the old site of the original Temple of Solomon. They had, being the innovative people they are, designed a portable altar they would carry to the holy spot in small pieces. The altar consisted of highly polished tubes of aluminum that fitted together in minutes without tools or connectors of any sort.

For the first time in over a thousand years, the Hebrews would have the privilege to sacrifice the life of a lamb to their God. All Israel and indeed Jewish peoples all over the world were caught up in a religious fever that reflected the importance the event held in their beliefs. It was all to take place in two more short days.

Bradley knew that somehow, for some reason he couldn't yet fathom, Brother would make himself visible again the day of the services in Jerusalem. He was probably traveling at that moment, just as Bradley and thousands of others were, to the city upon which the consciousness of the religious world was focused.

Bradley put down the paper and once again switched off his light. He leaned the seat back and tried to relax his overly taut muscles.

All the hotels were full. Bradley wanted to stay at the famous King David, but his feeble attempt at bribing the desk clerk had failed embarrassingly. At the Hilton an hour later his offer was much less feeble. When the absolutely full hotel yielded yet one more room he wondered if it was the increased amount he offered or the integrity of the men with whom he dealt.

The tiny room smelled of new paint and the multitude of varied colored throw rugs on the bare concrete floor attested to the fact that the room had indeed been unavailable only hours before. Bradley only cared about the bed. The flight and long wait for a room had drained him of all his energy. He let the bellman hang his clothes then turned him out with a large tip. He lay on top of the bed without removing his clothing and fell immediately into a deep sleep.

While Michael Bradley lay unconscious in his hotel room in the heart of the holy city, Sharon Klein was arriving at the home of her mother's sister in the suburban district of Mevasseret. She had, accompanied by her mother, flown to Jerusalem specifically to be present at the reinstitution of the sacrifice at the temple site.

The city was swelling at an alarming rate. Not only the hotels and restaurants of the tourism industry were being taxed, tens of thousands of the faithful were now staying with relatives and friends who lived in proximity to the city. Municipal services were being overloaded by the huge demands of the suddenly overpopulated area surrounding the mount. People camped openly in the streets without the necessary sanitary facilities. On the night before the Sabbath, localized electrical blackouts and interruptions of the potable water supply occurred almost continuously. When first light shone above the mountainous terrain the ancient city occupied, a third of the metropolitan area lacked one or another of these vital services.

When Bradley awoke after his twelve hour sleep with muscles cramped and joints stiff, his room and all the rooms at the expensive hotel lacked electricity and the water pressure was so low that bathing was impossible. Bradley's room was dark as night — he hadn't realized in his fatigue of the evening before that the room was on the interior of the hotel and, therefore, lacked sunlight.

He felt his way to the small bath to find that the faucets would supply only random trickles of flow. He tried the phone and it was also out of service. His temper flared momentarily until he remembered the thousands of people he had passed on his way from the airport. The sight of so many pilgrims lying in the streets had only aroused his curiosity at the time, but now he gleaned the reality of their numbers. The city was hopelessly overburdened by them. He wondered if the restaurant would be open to the guests when he felt the dull pain of hunger.

After leaving his dark room, he smoothed his wrinkled clothing in the soft yellow light of candles that had been placed at either end of the hallway. Other people were leaving their rooms, some sourly berating the hotel and all its employees, but most were laughing and joking as if they had been awarded an unexpected holiday.

There was a bellman in the stairwell conveying the guests down to the ground floor with a powerful flashlight. He apologized for the inconvenience in one breath, then condemned the massive influx of tourists with his next.

The restaurant was well lit with a multitude of windows, and a large buffet was brightly illuminated by battery powered fluorescent fixtures. The food consisted of cold sandwiches and Sterno-warmed soup. Bradley ate the meager offering with grateful gusto. When he attempted to pay the overly submissive waitress, he was informed that "Hilton International would not hear of an inconvenienced guest paying for sandwiches." He tipped the girl generously then asked her for some candles for his dark room.

At the stairwell, he decided not to wait for the next convoy to the upper floors and ignited one of the half dozen candles he had been given. At the second floor he began to accumulate a following. By the time he reached his own level, he was accompanied by a small throng of people from almost as many nations who needed his candle light to continue upward. At his floor he relinquished his responsibility as torch bearer to the nearest and opened the steel fire door to the sufficiently lighted hallway.

While he fumbled with his key, he thought about the rag tag appearance he must have made in the dining room. He was wondering about his soiled clothing when the opening door allowed a thin triangle of feeble light to penetrate the blackened room. Then as he stood in the doorway, a wave of emotion carried him back to the Mojave Desert and he remembered another episode of lightness-darkness and suddenly he felt naked.

He delayed at the threshold for only a moment, only the time it takes to fumble for a match, but the brief deferment was sufficient. He was hit in the chest by a huge shoulder; vice like arms encircled him and the two men flew across the semi-dark hallway to crash into the far wall.

Bradley's head slammed the plaster board with enough force to crush a circular hole in the flimsy material. His momentary dizziness cleared to find his right hand pulling at a meaty claw that covered his face, pushing his head into the depression made in the wall. His left hand stung with warm wetness, he forced his view to see the hand entwined around the bottom edge of a long razor being held a few inches from his throat. Bradley slammed a knee into the groin of his assailant without effect, then released the hand smashing his face so he could get both of his hands on the bigger problem of the razor. He couldn't see his attacker, but he could feel that by using of both of his hands against the assassin's single weapon arm he could pull the razor from him. Although the assailant was stronger than Bradley, he was being neutralized.

The hand left his face and Bradley rolled to the floor, pulling and twisting the hand and wrist he held with all the strength he had remaining. He felt the tearing in the still unseen elbow and the arm he clasped went limp. The razor came loose into Bradley's bloody left hand. He shifted his weight so he was, for the first time, above his attacker. The man was very large and muscular, his damaged right arm lay listlessly at his side, but his left arm struggled with frenzied energy in Bradley's stronger right-handed grasp.

Bradley looked at him for the first time as he brought the already dripping weapon to the man's neck. He was a square featured, good looking, olive skinned man near Bradley's own age. The high cheekbones told Bradley the identity of the one who would have surely killed him had he entered the dark room immediately upon opening the door.

"You're Yazzee, aren't you?" Bradley pushed the blade against the Indian's skin when he delayed his answer.

"Yes . . . I'm Yazzee."

"You killed Wilson?"

"Yes, it was ordered."

"And Barkman and Stone?"

"Yes, the Savior desired it."

"Where is he? Where is the one called Brother?"

"Never! You have won . . . kill me. I will never betray the Savior!" The big Indian suddenly turned inward as if he were listening intently to voices only he could hear. "He will meet you, in the old city — at the old market place."

Bradley was surprised at the change from non-negotiable resistance to passive submission, but before he could question his prisoner further, the Indian's right arm shot upward as if it had never been damaged. His right hand clamped on Bradley's left fist and wrist, pulling the razor he held to the Indian's throat closer, and then began to drag the blade deeply across the soft tissue of his own neck. Bradley pulled away with all his strength, but Yazzee held his hand on the handle of the razor beneath his vice-like fingers. The flesh parted and long spurts of blood rushed outward. Bradley began to retch and the Indian laughed quietly until the sharp edge severed his trachea.

The body went slack and Bradley stood as he dropped the deadly razor. Bile filled his throat with the acidic products of a stomach unable to withstand reality in its harshness. He walked down the hallway to the stairwell in a rapidly fading cloudiness of mind. The Indian had said that the one he had been pursuing would meet him where? In the old part of the city, but where? By the time he had stumbled down the stairs to the ground floor, his adrenalin caused turbidity of thought had cleared and he knew he had to get to the marketplace in the old part of the crowded city.

While Bradley pushed his way through the mass of humanity that clogged the streets of Jerusalem, Sharon Klein and her family were in the midst of the same swirling mob. They were very close to the temple mount, having departed for the Sabbath during the night so they could be sure to get to the sacrifice in time. After traveling so many miles, Sharon and her mother did not want to be late to the religious event of the millennia.

At the bazaar, Bradley was stunned by the confusion. He had thought the narrow stone streets of the old city had been the epitome of disorder, but the market was chaos. Arab vendors were wild with greed as they sold their goods at ridiculously inflated prices to the throngs of tourists that had infected their small shops and even smaller booths. Bradley despaired of ever meeting any one person in this carnival riot of infinite entropy.

Then he saw him, not twenty meters away; he was waving to him with a thin boned arm. Bradley moved slowly in the boy's direction and he disappeared into the crowd. Bradley moved to the point where he had last seen the white skinned adolescent with long, wavy blond hair standing and looked around in a slow inventory of the surrounding area. He saw him again. He was closer this time and

Bradley pushed people aside violently as he struggled to catch up with him.

So it went, each time Bradley forced his way to the point where the boy had last been, he was always just a little further ahead. Bradley at last grasped the rules of the game and slowed down. For no matter how fast or slow he followed, the boy was always the same distance ahead, laughing and waving. The boy led him down the stone paved streets that were hardly wider than the hallways in the hotel he had fled so unpremeditatedly. Their path took them up steep hills and through historic gates of ancient stone placed into precarious archways. Then, finally, the boy waved from the doorway of a shop before he slipped inside.

Bradley again rushed his gait, pushing people with both fists, leaving bloody stains on their garments with his bleeding left hand. Inside the shop, the customers and shopkeepers alike ignored his shouted inquiries as to the whereabouts of his prey. He crashed through the overly stocked goods without anyone seeming to notice him. He tore the curtain to the rear of the shop from its rusty wire rod and emerged into a sparsely furnished back room that was obviously used to entertain customers interested in less innocent commodities. Brother sat on an old wooden chair at the far side of the tiny stone room.

"Hello, Mickey, let me attend your wounds." Bradley's hand tingled for short seconds and the gaping slice was suddenly gone. He looked from his hand to the boy and back to his hand. He made the appendage, which had been almost useless before, into a tight fist covered with dried blood.

"Ah . . . I have amazed you. Many will be amazed before this day is gone." Bradley looked back up to the innocent looking youth with hate.

"Not if I kill you first."

"So you have guessed my intentions for the sacrifice today. But Mickey, you really should not harbor malice for the coming Savior." His smile brought a short lived reaction from Bradley. One step toward the boy and his legs froze into inactivity. He no longer had control over his own movements. He spit at the boy, but the spittle stopped in midflight and reversed trajectory to strike him on the cheek. He tried to speak, to curse at the lounging youth that had killed so many without compunction, but he found he could not force a sound.

"Relax Mickey, you are now under my protection. I have brought you here so you may know the entire truth. So I might meet you as a friend and thank you for all you have done. If you will be civil, I will allow you to speak." Bradley felt the muscles of his throat return to his control.

"I have never helped you . . . never."

"Oh, but you have. At the laboratory in Libya. Don't you remember? You were most helpful to me."

"I destroyed it. I destroyed the secret of selective genocide. How did that help you?"

"Oh, don't be so naive. You destroyed nothing!"

"It's gone. I saw it blow up . . . and I'll never tell you what little I know about how they did it."

"If I wanted you to, you would, but it's not necessary. There is another laboratory. My people there have viruses that can destroy almost any race I choose, whenever I choose." Bradley was sickened. He thought only of the needless murder of the Richardsons.

"Why? What was the point?"

"The point, Mickey, was fusion. Molecular fusion. The time is coming when I will need weaponry far superior to any now known to the rest of the world. There is a war coming, you know. I intend to win this war . . . for the good of all mankind, of course."

"Molecular fusion?" Bradley exhaled the bitter breath of one totally defeated. "You know about that?"

"Know about it . . . it was my idea in the first place. Only my scientists couldn't make the theory a reality. That is why I contrived to have you help me. You were by far the best inorganic chemist, you know. I needed that one indefinable, illogical, unpredictable instant of genius. I needed someone who could bridge the gap in our logic that had stymied our work. You, Mickey, supplied that moment of genius. My people are now synthesizing the molecular catalyst by the kilogram."

Bradley's head slumped to his chest and when he spoke, he was very, very quiet.

"You're him. You're really him. I didn't believe it until now . . . I didn't believe in any of it, but it was all true. They all knew about you. You're really him."

"Certainly I am, Mickey. But you need to realize that I am but a product of all of you." His eyes seemed to focus at a spot above Bradley's head. "Well, the ritual is starting, so I really must be going. It wouldn't due to be late, so good-bye my reluctant friend." Bradley felt a piercing pain in his chest as his heart stopped functioning. He was young and strong, so he didn't die quickly, but he did, eventually, stop living.

Mount Moriah was a strange synthesis of the extremely old and the extremely new. The multitudes of faithful had come to see and participate in an age old ritual and the media had come to broadcast that ritual worldwide via satellite.

The hundreds of thousands present and the hundreds of millions watching on television around the world witnessed the ritual as they had expected it to proceed. A lamb had been offered at the only site in the world where such an offering could, by the ancient teachings, be legitimately sacrificed. But as soon as the lamb's blood had been taken and it was being prepared for the sacrificial pyre, a disturbance occurred. It wasn't a violent disturbance; it was instead a wave of emotion that followed a slight, blonde haired youth on his slow passage through the multitude.

He was garbed in white linen and he smiled innocently as he followed his slow trek to the portable altar. As he progressed ever closer, he filled the worshippers with euphoria and stopped to cure the ills of the sick. He was strangely unmolested as he neared his destination. Then, when he reached the altar where all proceedings had ceased during his healing procession, he spoke with a voice that was heard by all in attendance clearly and in their native tongues.

"It is good that you worship me. But the sacrifice of an innocent lamb's life is not necessary to obtain my approval." And with this sentence the dead lamb jumped to its feet on the shining altar. It leaped down and ran conspicuously about the altar area before running into the crowd of awed worshippers. "I am the one you have so patiently awaited — I give you my love." Everyone in attendance and millions watching on television felt his love.

The one called Brother descended from the altar and again went into the audience to cure the feeble. After an hour he departed from the mount as suddenly as he had appeared.

When the old Rabbis leading the ritual knelt in prayer and thanks, the tens of thousands of worshippers were overcome with tearful ecstasy. Sharon Klein at that moment felt the powerful drive of a calling; she silently devoted the rest of her life to the service of the Savior. She felt that her life to this point had been preparation for this commitment. She felt lucky to have been in the throng of worshipers when the Savior had at last come back to his chosen people.

Author's Note

*S*pirit of Error was written very early in my career, before the course of my life had been determined. My dream had always been to write fiction, but my education had taken a somewhat unintended turn toward science. I had finished my degree in biochemistry and was working as a Post Graduate Research Chemist at the University of California, Riverside. In those days, the late seventies, there was an explosion of knowledge occurring in the fields of microbiology and biochemistry and I was in the middle of it. The convoluted plot of *Spirit* began with the realization that specific racial identities could be selectively attacked in a genetic war.

When my research director made the subtle suggestion that I enter a doctorate program in chemistry I knew the jig was up. It had been a great job while it lasted, but a few more lonely years cloistered in a chemistry laboratory would not get me the life experiences I needed to write. I soon learned that his subtle suggestion came just ahead of unemployment, which is where I landed soon after avoiding the commitment. Then like now the economy was in a downturn and leaving the university was a shock to my pocketbook.

I wrote the bulk of *Spirit* in 1979 while working as an itinerate bartender, traveling across America in a van, and much of it while

233

working on Bourbon Street in New Orleans. After my van exploration of America, I returned to my tiny hometown of Barstow in the middle of the Mojave Desert. There in a sunny cold room I brought *Spirit* together in a single hand written document. That was 1980.

During the time I worked on *Spirit* our country was not optimistic about America's role in the future. We had lost the Vietnam War after a televised decade of death, we had experienced not one but two oil shortages, and we had watched impotently as our embassy staff in Iran was paraded, bound and blindfolded, in front of the world. The Middle East had suffered through another deadly war only a few years before and by the end of the decade it had become widely accepted that weapons of mass destruction had been introduced into that fragile political environment.

The first typed draft of *Spirit* came along once I moved to Long Beach in 1981. There a sweet and generous neighbor performed the heroic task of translating hundreds of crumpled loose pages of nearly indecipherable penmanship into a single typed document. Thank you, Joann, wherever you may be.

In 1982 I worked briefly with a screen writer to produce a screen play from the story. Although otherwise unproductive, it was quite heady, when lunching in a Santa Monica restaurant frequented by the power élite of Hollywood, to be referred to for the first time as "the Author."

After the ego boosting, but unfruitful screen play experience, *Spirit* became baggage. The first drafts were stuffed into an old soft-vinyl briefcase and forgotten. I pursued a career in chemical engineering that took me around the world: Los Angeles, Honolulu, Manila, Shanghai, Bangkok, Baden, Abidjan, Philadelphia, San Francisco, and finally back to Manhattan Beach. By the year 2000 *Spirit* was just one of three unpublished manuscripts buried in the collected flotsam and jetsam of a life spent traveling.

In 2009 I happened to reread *Spirit* and was again caught up in the story. Many of today's headlines mirror the plot lines within *Spirit* and today's conflicts in the Middle East could easily be written into it without anachronism. I realized that although it is unpolished, *Spirit* still has political and scientific relevance.

Spirit of Error is printed here as it has existed since late 1979. It has been edited for grammar and in some cases sentence clarity. No changes have been made to the book's structure, plot or characters. I hope the story, as topical today as it has ever been, can overcome the less artistic aspects of the book.

James J. Houts
Valencia, CA
20 March 2011

www.ingramcontent.com/pod-product-compliance
Lightning Source LLC
Chambersburg PA
CBHW070601130626
46556CB00001B/234